BACK EAST

BACK
EAST

by Ellen Pall

David R. Godine · Boston

First published in 1983 by

David R. Godine, Publisher, Inc.
306 Dartmouth Street
Boston, Massachusetts 02116

Library of Congress Cataloging in Publications Data

Pall, Ellen 1952–
  Back East.
  I. Title.
PS3566.A463B3   1983   813'.54   82–49345
ISBN 0–87923–477–6

First printing
Printed in the United States of America

For Helen, who brought me up to read,
Daddy, who taught me diligence,
and in loving remembrance of my mother,
this book.

As there are a thousand thoughts
lying within a man that he does
not know till he takes up the pen
to write, so the heart is a secret
even to him (or her) who
has it in his own breast.

—WILLIAM MAKEPEACE THACKERAY,
Henry Esmond

BACK EAST

ONE

❧❧

IN MY FAMILY when someone decides to do you a favor it's best to cooperate. Therefore I let my brother Jules pick me up at JFK. Jules had taken the most peculiar attitude toward my coming back east. A person would almost think he wished to discourage me.

On the phone the previous May he'd told me I'd be miserable in New York. I listened without much interest. Summer in Southern California is one long held breath. A hint of the coming stagnancy hung like a haze in the warm afternoon. I was lying upside-down on my bed, a wet glass of ice-water in one outflung hand. The phone receiver rested in the other, just touching the tip of my ear. Jules's voice flowed from the earpiece, trickled through my tangled hair and spread out across the sheets. My legs were propped up on the wall so high my feet had gone numb. I rolled toward the window onto my side and curled up around the receiver, crushing it under my ear. The ice in the dripping ice-water shifted and clinked as I lifted it over myself. I set it on the flowered bedsheet inches from my eyes. Through the streaming condensation I could see a hummingbird

3

swiftly stab an orange blossom. Summer was coming like the chorus of a Beach Boys song.

"Jules," I said, "I've got to get out of here."

"Well." His voice poked at my ear now, sharp and thin as the wire that carried it. "I can get that place in the West Village for you, if you really think you're coming."

"I'm coming." Magnified and yellowish where they pressed against the glass, waterlogged, clumsy, my fingers started to lose their feeling. My ear was crumpled against the receiver.

"It's expensive, don't forget. The lease still runs a year and a half. According to Daphne the landlord is reasonable and the place is quiet, except for she says the pipes make a lot of noise. Still want it?"

"Absolutely." My lips kissed the plastic mouthpiece.

"She won't be leaving until July."

"Jesus."

"Change your mind?"

"No. But I have to be up in Maine in August."

"You don't have to take it. I told her I'd let her know tomorrow."

"Tell her I want it."

Jules hesitated. On the line the static rose and fell. It gave a climactic lurch, then died. "Listen Melanie," he asked at last, "are you sure you've thought this through? I see people come here from L.A. all the time, thinking they'll like it. Nobody stays."

"Jules, I'm *from* New York—"

"Yes but this isn't Sands Point," he broke in. "This is the city. It's different. I don't like it."

"Huh?"

"The way you've decided to come here so suddenly. I

4

don't like it. You ought to consider it."

"It's not so sudden, believe me. I've been thinking about it for months now."

"Well. But L.A.'s been good for you. You've been happy there. I don't think you should come."

My attention shifted again to the open window. Through the column of glass and water the world outside seemed a pleasant aquarium. Dark blurry leaves waved gently, blotting the sunlight. Birds swam through the bright, peaceful, undulant air. My focus reverted to my yellowish fingers. I could see the circling grooves in them plainly. I licked a drop of water off the glass with the tip of my tongue. "I haven't been happy here," I said.

"I thought you were."

"Now you know."

I could tell Jules was shaking his head in frustration. An Armour believes he knows best about everything. I understood.

"Would you rather I didn't come?" I asked, just wondering.

His voice returned sounding as if it had been ironed flat. "I'm only concerned for your sake."

"Well thank you. I'll take my chances, okay?"

"Okay," he said, but added after a moment, "You know, I think Mother was just finally getting ready to visit you out there."

"Hey," I said. "Maybe some other life cycle."

"Sure."

I rolled over on my back again, closing my eyes. My water glass left a damp puddle on the sheets. "Will you send me the lease?"

"I'll have Daphne send it."

"I appreciate this."

"Let me know what time your flight gets in."

"Oh, you don't have to—"

"Just let me know. I'll pick you up."

"But I'd—"

"Talk to you later," said Jules. He hung up.

He was still pretty doleful three months later when he came for me at the airport. My spirits had improved. We embraced after a fashion and jaunted off in a cab to the city. I threw a few bright openers his way and now and then he returned a weary glance, as if to say he'd seen hundreds of sisters move to New York and no good had ever come of it yet. The air in the city was soft and dirty, like a favorite quilt whose day has gone by.

Jules unlocked the empty apartment and handed me the key. It was pretty much as I'd pictured it, large and quiet, with the living room, dining room, and kitchen upstairs, where you come in, and two bedrooms and a walled garden below. We turned on the lights and the air conditioning. I walked around it, taking inventory. Daphne had left me not only her bed and refrigerator and stove but also:

Light fixtures

Green towels

Green soap

Green toilet paper

Phone books

On the bed, starry, unwashed Peter Max sheets

A plastic lamp with a lime colored shade and

A ceramic toothbrush holder in the shape of a jolly frog.

"Your friend Daphne seems to have this thing about green," I observed, running my finger along the low windowsill in the living room. It left a fat streak of white in the dust.

He didn't exactly reply. "You okay?" he asked.

"Yes. Fine." I smiled. I broke briefly into a time-step to demonstrate my competence.

"Terrific. The phone should still be hooked up. Call me tomorrow and we'll have dinner. Enjoy yourself."

He left.

The air conditioner shifted into a higher gear; its throaty hum reverberated through the living room. I looked out the front window: Jules was already gone. Across the street a youngish couple stood in the doorway of their apartment making plans, each of them gesturing with a full set of keys.

I was alone at last. My adventure was launched; I was off and running, or sailing, or flying, or what you will. In anticipation I had figured attractively at this point in the daydream as a sort of magician about to pull a live bunny-rabbit out of a demonstrably empty hat. Suddenly I was the bunny, untimely ripped from my secret pouch. I faltered. I glanced into each room again after Jules had left. I locked the front door. I looked out each window. I succumbed to a tide of misery.

I turned out the lights. I went down the stairs, undoing my skirt. I stepped out of it, took off my sandals, turned out the lamp. Unwashed, still in my shirt, my suitcases unopened in the living room above me, I crawled in between the dingy Peter Max sheets and rested my head on the mattress. There was no pillow. The air in the bedroom was warm and stale. City sounds drifted around me. This is my home now, I thought. I slid down my sadness as if it were a chute, life at the top end, sleep at the bottom. As I fell I wondered how that trick with the rabbits got started. Magicians produce them with such pride and flourish you'd think the audience had been crying, "Rabbit! Rabbit! Rabbit!" all evening.

TWO

※

THE NEXT DAY I met Lucian.

I woke up feeling better. A great deal remains to be written about the therapeutic effects of morning. The bedroom was full of light now, the more so as there were no curtains. I lay in bed, head heavy on my folded hands, and contemplated my new domain. Patches of Spackle floated like splotchy clouds on the white walls. In the sun that swept the hardwood floor I could make out where Daphne's rugs had been and where they hadn't. Though the air conditioner was still audible upstairs the air in the bedroom was so old and thick I felt I could hardly breathe. There was a sliding door between me and the garden. I slithered out from between the sad sheets and opened it all the way. The morning was fragrant and still and bright. I stepped outside to wiggle my toes on the dusty, sun-warm bricks of the patio. An elderly woman came out on a balcony up to my left. I ducked back inside, leaving the glass door open in hopes of a breeze, went upstairs for my suitcases and down again, and headed for the bathroom.

Though I had never met her, Daphne was my first real company in that apartment. I saw her all over. Upstairs I paused at the long, low dining room windows to look down into the garden. I imagined her standing in the same place before me. When I used the toilet I thought of her sitting there. Brushing my teeth, spitting into the sink, I thought of her bending and spitting. I saw her face in the frame of the mirror. I put my toothbrush where hers had been, washed with her soap, dried with her towels. I imagined her streetwise and practical, talented, pretty. The life she had lived in this apartment was a challenge and model to me. I must live up to her level.

On the way to breakfast I tried to remember which streets went which way. I'd been in New York often before but the Village still confused me. It was a Wednesday. The streets near my house were sleepy and quiet. Then I blundered onto Seventh Avenue. I scurried back out of the way in alarm, retreating to find shelter in a tiny coffee shop. Over eggs and coffee I read the *New York Times*. When I'd slept and fed, as Tennyson might say, I began to look to the matter of hoarding. I made a list of things to buy in a spiral notebook I had in my purse. In a dramatic and altogether gratuitous gesture I'd sold nearly everything I owned before departing L.A. My list ran three pages by the time I left the coffee shop. I wandered around the Village a little, bought some groceries, got lost. Then I went home to Daphne's apartment—mine now—and arranged my belongings on the shelves.

My profession, if the term still applies, is writing songs. I'm a songwriter. That's what I did in L.A. I first went there to major in music at UCLA. I had a vague idea of being a composer, I think, or maybe a music teacher. This all sounds like somebody else's life to me now, but the fact is my second quarter there I wrote a song as homework for a class. The assignment was to write a rock 'n' roll song where the bass line was the hook. This was early in 1969. My song was called "Dawn of Love." A classmate of mine liked it, a singer. She dropped out soon after to cut a record. She put "Dawn of Love" on her record. The record never went anywhere much but a filmmaker heard it who was making an antiwar movie. This is now 1970. The filmmaker liked "Dawn of Love" so much he made it the theme song of his movie. He also called the movie *Dawn of Love*. Because some of the performers in it got to be famous later on this movie is still shown sometimes. In 1971 it was kind of a cult film. At that point an executive from Helicon Music saw it. He liked the song. He found me and signed me to a publishing contract. I dropped out of school and became a songwriter.

I stayed with Helicon—the publishing end of Pelion Records—and wrote what they asked for. This was fine. Except for an occasional tune written as a gift, or with intent to seduce, my idea of personal expression at the time was to snort coke and race down Mulholland Drive. Preferably imperiling others. If I had no aesthetics, I had all the anesthetics a girl could ask for. I wasn't a deep thinker. I wrote anti-establishment songs of Rage. I wrote songs about love, Jesus, commitment, despair, songs about songs. It didn't matter. I wrote strictly on assignment, which of course suited Helicon down to the ground. When disco showed up I wrote a song for them called "Real Life." They gave it to Gloria Mack and she cut it. It hit the charts at twenty-seven with a bullet. After that—this was '75—they mainly expected disco from me. It got so I hated disco after a while.

This is maybe as much as I need to say about my career

till then. Sometimes it didn't go too well and I fell back on
money I had inherited from my father. After a while I got
fairly tired of L.A. Some of my friends died and I gave up
drugs for the most part. I was lonely all the time. I lived
with a series of rock 'n' roll musicians—a good way to stay
lonely, doubtless. I have a slight tendency to get involved
with difficult people so I don't have to think about myself.
Especially handsome male difficult people. I've done it
again and again.

Altogether I stayed in L.A. some twelve years. Twelve
years of anything I think is plenty. However, tired as I
was at the end of it, I didn't know what to do with myself.
If I'd had any values I might have returned to my values;
but I didn't have any. I didn't know anything to do except
leave for a different place. New York seemed like a challenge. So I went back east.

My first morning there continued promisingly. By the
time I left my new home again I was feeling fairly frisky.
I went to A-1 Keyboard to rent a piano and even shuffled
an impromptu soft shoe to a little Fats Waller another
customer played. The salespeople clapped. I bowed and
made my exit.

In a froth of bonhomie I arrived by cab at Helicon Music. Helicon's east coast offices are on the thirtieth and
thirty-first floors of one of those huge shiny black build-
ings, those architectural Darth Vaders, that increasingly
menace Manhattan. My appointment was with Patty Bates,
whom I had met once or twice at parties in L.A., and who
was now to be my contact at Helicon. She was a small
plaster-colored woman about my age, with a sweet, tiny
face; behind her huge chrome and walnut desk she appeared not quite life-sized but more like a large doll. The

tight swaths of black leather that banded the steely chairs around her seemed in her demure presence to suggest a sexual fetish. I sat in one of those low black chairs with an obscure sense of having fallen into a basket. I'd come into the building overheated; the thin mist of perspiration on my cheeks and forehead now seemed to freeze into a flaky, fragile lacquer.

"It's nice to see you again," said Patty, looking over the huge high desk as a child peeks over a counter.

"Thank you."

"I'm sure we'll work well together."

I became aware of the soles of my feet, which still stuck slightly to the worn leather soles of my sandals. My toes were cold and damp. The room seemed to be refrigerated. Patty wore a sweater. She appeared to have to nerve herself even to achieve cordiality; really she looked as if she'd have liked to run away.

"I had a call from Dick Adair just yesterday," she said.

"Did you?"

"Yes." She smiled, and her hopeful eyes glinted at me. She had a habit, perhaps the result of timidity, of waiting between her phrases for you to say uh-huh or oh or mmm or to answer her, so as to make you punctuate her speech.

"Oh," I said.

"He thought I might have seen you already."

"But you hadn't," I suggested.

"No. He was looking for that Enright song." She smiled apologetically. How had she managed to get this job? I thought businesswomen had to be tough.

"Oh yes." Tommy Enright was waiting for a song from me.

"They go into the studio two weeks from next Tuesday."

"Oh. Really?"

"You will have it soon, won't you?" Apparently it distressed her to have to pressure me this way. I couldn't get away from the idea that all of this businesslike talk faintly embarrassed her.

"Absolutely. Almost finished."

"I'll give him a call back and tell him."

"Do that. Do that."

"He'll be relieved." She smiled again, helplessly, it seemed, and the friendliness in her eyes was like the call of a drowning man.

"I'm sure. Well—"

"Melanie, do you think we should discuss your contract? It expires October first, I think. . . ." She broached the subject reluctantly, as a girl's mother might bring up birth control or menstruation. Maybe it was the association, or perhaps I had a moment of prescience, but all at once I couldn't stay there talking with her any longer.

I blurted out, "No, I have to go," and jumped up from my chair. I felt as if Patty's manner had infected me. I grinned at her lamely. "We can discuss it later, I mean—if that's okay. Okay?" I fumbled for my purse. I didn't understand why Patty and I couldn't shake off our roles and speak normally. She seemed to be trying so hard, and I was more than game. Suddenly the spectacle of her goodwill straining across that desk and always falling short was more than I could take.

"Will you give me a call when you're settled?"

"For sure." I felt horribly defeated, as if there were no love in the world. I reached the door, then had to go back to shake her hand. She stood up too. I've never really gotten used to shaking women's hands. Patty's was cool and delicate, her grip listless.

"I'll go out with you," she said.

"Oh fine."

"I'm going to lunch." She made a final attempt. "Would you like to join me?" She took an umbrella that leaned in a corner behind her desk. Why? She'd had one before when I met her too; it flashed through my mind that she might have been born with one, the way some babies are born clutching IUDs.

Cravenly, I said, "Thank you but I can't."

"Well then . . . next time, maybe."

"Oh for sure." She gave me a new smile, in which a little of our common failure was acknowledged, and followed me out past the receptionist's desk to the bank of elevators. We stood and waited. The truth gently faded from her eyes and soon I squirmed again under her gaze. It was curious and friendly, like a sightseer's.

An elevator opened at last, several people already in it. One, Patty told me, was Walter Preisler, Helicon's new east coast vice president. Behind him a young man stood in profile to me. He was listening to us I thought.

"This is Melanie Armour," Patty announced to Preisler, a tall, fortyish man with a wonderful set of sideburns that he might have ordered from Hammacher Schlemmer. He had a nervous habit of licking his lips with his flat, dry tongue before speaking. "She's just moved here from L.A., you know. She'll be keeping in touch with our office now."

"Oh yes. I think I heard about that. Well! Welcome."

"Thank you."

"Where are you living? Find an apartment yet?"

"Yes. My brother found one for me."

"Oh? That was lucky. Are you two going to lunch?" Walter Preisler beamed heartily at me and Patty. The elevator stopped, opened, shut and started again. It dropped with an eerie noiselessness. Though I do not like personable or quirky elevators, this one was disconcertingly neutral.

"No, Melanie can't."

I felt called upon to explain, lest Patty suffer for my desertion. That much kindness there was in me.

"I have a million things to do," I said. "New place and all."

The elevator was descending with excruciating deliberateness. I exchanged a cowardly, sheepish glance with Patty. We stopped at nearly every floor. People moved on and off, mostly on. It got crowded. The listening man was pushed a little nearer me. I could see him better now. He was hardly more than a boy, really, a man-boy, tall and graceful. Extremely handsome. The kind of perfection I tend to forget occurs in the species at all. When it comes to beauty in men I have the sexual equivalent of a sweet tooth. I wanted to study him uninterrupted but corporate protocol forbade it. It was necessary that we all continue to talk until we parted. Otherwise the encounter would have been a failure.

"I didn't realize your brother lived in New York," said Patty.

"Oh yes. He's a critic for the *Beat*. Theater critic. Jules Armour."

"Isn't that something? That's quite a talented family you have there," said Preisler, in the tone you might use to remark on a child's model airplane collection.

"Oh yes," Patty confirmed. She appeared to know me much better all of the sudden. I hated her for this treachery: at least in her office we had both been palpably awkward. The elevator crawled down the shaft. "Are your parents in the arts too Melanie?"

The beautiful man-boy turned his head slightly. Past

Walter Preisler's regulation gray temple I could see him in three-quarter view. Delicious.

"No. My father was a businessman. Paper products."

"Oh." She tactfully ignored the Was. "And your mother? Does she live in the city?"

There was a theatrical agency on the floor above Helicon's offices. That must be where the man-boy came from. My own voice hummed like white noise in my ears, vibrating uselessly. "No, my mother lives in Maine. As a matter of fact, I'm going up there in a few days to stay for a month. She wants me to help look after my niece."

Fear startled Patty into matter-of-factness. "But the song—" she said. "Will you have time?"

The elevator was now drifting past the fourth floor. The man-boy abruptly turned to face me. Hitherto I couldn't even be sure he had seen me but now he stood dead across from my face and looked me straight in the eyes. It gave me the most peculiar sensation—as if he had stepped inside me. He turned away with the faintest smile.

I reassured Patty about the song as the lobby arrived. We parted at last, with much shaking of hands. I had lost interest in both Patty and Preisler. I said I'd remembered a phone call and lingered in the lobby while they took themselves off. I was sorry to see the man-boy vanish too. I waited a minute, sealed up in a phone booth, then pushed through the heavy revolving door of the building.

Traffic growled; heat roared. A flood of strangers sluiced the sidewalks. I sank back into the very next door, a few steps down the dazzling white pavement. I found myself in an empty luncheonette lighted with long fluorescent tubes and smelling strongly of air conditioning. My excursion into the street had been so brief it sounded like a

window opened on a train in a tunnel and shut again before you can say Shut the window.

There weren't any tables here. The counter was one of
those zigzaggy designer's inspirations consisting of four or
five Formica peninsulas ranged across the steamy white
sandbar of the kitchen. I sat on the stool at the inmost edge
of the farthest peninsula from the door. I ordered tea and
took out my spiral notebook. When I looked up I found
that my beautiful fellow elevator passenger was sitting across
from me, looking straight at me.

We didn't speak. I smiled but he didn't smile back,
though his eyes again looked directly into me. He ordered
coffee: his voice was young and polite and conspicuously
devoid of an accent. He watched the waitress, refusing to
meet my eyes again. She came with his cup and he paid
right away. He took a few swallows, glanced inquiringly
at me once before I quite had time to catch him and look
back, and left. I left soon after.

I went home on the subway, determined to behave like
a real New Yorker. My visit to Helicon had succeeded in
reminding me Tommy Enright's song couldn't be put
off forever. Pleased with myself for finding my own way,
relieved to discover my street still quiet and my apartment
cool, I dug up the notebook I'd written half the lyrics in
and started to come up with the rest. I didn't like working without a piano but I had brought a little cassette recorder with me from Los Angeles, so at least I could sing
onto it and hear what I had back. After a while I phoned
Jules and he told me to show up at his place at six. I didn't
have a watch. I had to keep dialing Time.

It's depressing to write lyrics for a disco song. You know
nobody's going to listen to them. By six o'clock I was

starving and tired, but at least I had the words completed. That cheered me up; and a good thing too, because when you go visiting in my family you want to bring your own smile and shoeshine.

I opened the door to leave and found my man-boy in the vestibule. Goodness knows I tried to be frightened. I thought how triumphant Jules would be if I got raped or killed my first day in the city. Anyway there are certain things it doesn't look well to take in stride. I asked him what he was doing there, trying to sound hostile.

His lips parted. Wonderful teeth. "I followed you," he said.

Hearing him say it I suddenly was scared. "I didn't think it was coincidence." I dropped back a little through my still-open door, thinking it might be wise to disappear.

"Don't be afraid," he advised. I am always getting swell advice like this from these terrific inside sources. I hovered on the threshold. "It's nothing like that."

"What's it like?"

"I just . . . I wanted to know you. I'm sorry."

"I don't—"

"My name is Lucian Curry." Abruptly he laughed. Smiled. He put out his hand for me to take and I took it. We shook hands. Mine burned like a fuse in his soft dry palm. "Look, I'm sorry, you must think I'm crazy—"

"Possibly."

"But I saw you in that office building and I couldn't just let you go."

"I beg your pardon?"

"I want to know you. I'd like to get to know you. I even sort of feel like I know you already. Didn't you feel it? I followed you all the way through the subway," he added wistfully. Wistful was a keynote with him. I couldn't hold out any longer.

Loosing my death grip on the doorknob I mumbled, "Look, I have to go out now. If you really—"

"I do know you, by the way," he broke in. "I mean I know you're a songwriter. I know your songs. You're Melanie Armour. You wrote 'Dawn of Love.'"

I am not now and have never been famous. I still don't know how Lucian happened to be familiar with my career—except that Lucian made a point of being aware of a lot of little things. "How in hell do you know that?"

He looked uncomfortable. "In the elevator," he said. "Your friend introduced you."

"My friend," I repeated. "Oh."

"But even before that I knew you were creative. I mean, I immediately had this feeling you were an artist." It will give you an idea how sweet and earnest and young he was when I say that in his mouth the word artist was not merely inoffensive but had a positive, if awkward, charm. I speak as a person who has lost her appetite at the very mention of Artists. His eyes stopped burning into mine and instead looked at me questioningly, eagerly. It was all past resisting.

"You're very young, aren't you," I said.

He smiled. "A little young."

"You would really like to know me?" He was extraordinarily beautiful.

"Yes, I would."

"Then," I said, feeling kindly and ancient, "why don't you come have breakfast with me at nine tomorrow? I have to go out now or we could have dinner."

"I would love to come," he said sweetly.

I locked my door. "Do you do this very often?" I asked. We walked up the street. He didn't answer. I looked and found his eyes serious, reproachful, disappointed. He would always, as I was to discover, respond to my frail attempts at humor this way. He thought them beneath me. He shook his head No. At the corner we stopped. Gravely he put out his hand. We shook again. I felt like Uncle Pumblechook bidding good-bye to Pip.

"Tomorrow at nine," he said. He turned the other way down the street. I'm sure that no matter which way I had taken he'd have gone the other. He had found the moment to make his exit. He really had nowhere particular to go.

❦

Dinner with Jules was rather more what I expected than what I could strictly like. Regarding my move to New York, he seemed to have taken a policy of being as dubious and difficult as he could. In childhood Jules was often my ally. He loved me I guess, and still does in the way Armours love each other, which is not much practical use. At present he had made up his mind I would be happier out of the city. He set out to make me feel this as acutely and painfully and often as possible. He cooked shrimp for me, to which he knows perfectly well I am allergic; and the meal was only the objective correlative, as T. S. Eliot might say, of the conversation. He chatted aggressively on topics he knows drive me crazy, especially the business interests left to the family by my father. These were then under the joint supervision of Jules and my father's longtime partner Norman Flexner. Jules and our older sister Iris and I used to call him No-No Norman on account of his attitude regarding advances of cash; but Jules's fluent references to him now intimated they were pals from Way Back. Jules also spoke at length of our mother. Espresso had barely dampened our demitasses when the doorbell rang and he remembered he had a show to see that evening. And a date. I got the message.

I arrived at my apartment—mine in deed only, ahem—feeling exiled but mulish. Daphne was with me from the moment I turned the key in the double-locked dead-bolted door. Inside, the telephone lurked in its smug plastic casing, a tie line to the past. I defied it. I planted myself on the floor with my lyrics, some music paper and a glass of sweet New York water. I penciled in the six notes I meant to use for the hook. They stared at me from the lines of the staff like the eyes of Gilbert and Sullivan's three little maids peeping over their fans. I sipped my water. I stared back at them. I could read, I thought. I could go out again. I studied the windows. They needed to be measured. Blinds should be ordered, lists should be made, there was meting and doling and all life, for goodness' sake, demanding that I take note of it. But I didn't want to think about that. I didn't want to think about disco. I wanted to think about young Lucian Curry. It would be fun to see him again. I thought I might write a song for him.

THREE

≫≪

LUCIAN SHOWED UP the next morning about ten o'clock. After a while I realized he ran on a kind of three-quarter-scale model of normal time. The piano arrived just before he did, so, as he pointed out, it was a good thing he hadn't been punctual. His arrival interrupted a phone call to my mother. I promised to call her again. Lucian looked rested and perfectly calm. "Are you always late?" I asked in my innocence, looking around for somewhere to put down the phone and finding no one place better than any other. Except for the newly installed piano, my living room was empty.

"No," he said. He was still wearing blue jeans, but yesterday's linen jacket had been replaced with a shirt of soft, faded, tiny plaid. What is this endless appetite I have for beauty? You would think I would get enough of it sometime. Lucian stood easily. He never leaned; he kept his weight on both feet equally.

"You can tell me," I encouraged.

"Yes." He smiled.

"How old are you?"

"Eighteen." His cheeks changed color. Something hot

and pink ran into them. I realized he was blushing. "Seventeen."

"Oh Jesus." I sighed. "Let's go eat breakfast."

We revisited my neighborhood coffee shop, Lucian questioning me intently about the piano, the apartment, how I'd slept—I don't know why. He wanted to know everything, that's how he was; it's a good trait. "I had a bad night myself," he at last confided.

"What happened?"

"Oh, nothing." He looked rueful and shook his head. He looked at me as if trying to figure out how smart I might be, what he could tell me.

"Somebody hurt you? Trouble on the home front?"

Shake shake shake. "Let's think about breakfast."

"Lucian, where do you live?"

"Central Park West. For the moment." He essayed a grim laugh.

"Alone?"

"Ah, no—"

"You have a—"

"Well now, tell me about this move to New York," he leaped in. "Why did you come back?"

"Change."

"But you go to Maine soon?"

"How did you know that?"

"In the elevator." He looked ghastly uncomfortable and started to spin the glass ashtray around and around with the tip of his long straight index finger. His nails were square and perfect, like a row of small pink panes.

"Oh yes."

"Did you say your folks are up there?"

"Mother. Where are your folks?"

"Indiana." He gave me a quick glance to see if this was all right with me. "Is it just your mother?"

"No; also my niece and her father." I tried to catch the waitress's eye, but she was gazing with dreamy malignance into the kitchen and didn't see me. She'd given us menus—long, oversized, laminated things with the moist greasy feel of something that's been wiped with a damp cloth. There was no one else in the whole place except a rumpled man at the counter, drinking tea and eating what looked like pie. I went on, "He'll be gone on sabbatical though when I'm up there. I'm only going for a month."

"Oh. Your niece is—your brother's child?"

"How did you know I had a brother?"

He looked profoundly embarrassed. The ashtray accelerated. "The elevator . . ."

"Oh. Dear me, I seem to have chatted my head off in that elevator," I said. "What else did I say?"

"Not much. So, your niece?"

"Oh yes. Megan. She's my sister's child. Listen, are there a lot more of these questions?"

"Where's your sister?"

"Dead. Buried. In Queens."

The ashtray stopped with a clatter. "And your father?"

"He's dead too. In Maine. We bury Armours where they fall—like soldiers."

"Oh. God." He almost put his hand out for mine, I saw him.

"This is a while ago," I said. He was looking embarrassed and taken aback, as if he'd been looking for a towel in my bathroom and found a prosthesis instead. "Seven or eight years ago," I reassured him. The waitress finally glanced at me and I waved at her encouragingly. She moseyed over. We ordered.

"We used to spend our summers in Maine," I said. "Then my parents moved up there permanently."

"What's your brother-in-law like?" he asked me.

"Saintly."

"Really?"

"I think. He lives with my mother. He's going to marry again soon, it looks like."

"Who?"

"Sharon Dennison. No one you know."

"Who is she?"

"She's a local girl up there. Mother isn't happy."

"She doesn't like her?"

"Not since marriage came up. This is from what I can gather."

"Is anything wrong with Sharon?"

Lucian watched me seriously. He took life absolutely seriously—something you can afford to do if you are very young I guess. Preferably very young and very beautiful. He never laughed except from embarrassment, or from excess of pleasure. "From my mother's point of view. She's young. Twenty or something. Donald's thirty-seven I guess."

"Oh."

"And an unwed mother. Or divorced—no that's right, she's an unwed mother. Plus—isn't this boring you?"

"No; I want to know."

"But why?"

He frowned impatiently. "I just do. Go on. What else?"

"She cleans house for my family. She has no education, not even a high school diploma . . ." As I talked I was becoming increasingly certain that Lucian was gay. I don't know what suggested it—nothing particular in his speech or manner—and it was hardly what I wished to conclude; but I had had a suspicion the day before, and now I was convinced. "You can't imagine what that means to my mother," I went on; "my mother is not the easiest woman in the world. And Donald's a college professor. Mother is something of a social climber. Or was in her day."

"Oh. And—?"

"Sharon's family runs Dennison's One-Stop in Webster. Combination grocery store and luncheonette. Great place." I closed my eyes. Under the smell of coffee-shop eggs came the scent of a certain kind of fine black hair, so fine it looked like thread on a spool, and felt like the tassels at the ends of a braided cord. "Oh gee," I breathed. "Dennison boys."

"What?"

"Dennison boys." I opened my eyes. "Sharon's brothers. They were older, my age—older. Many a cool summer eve have I warmed my poor frame over a Dennison boy. I wouldn't be surprised if Benjy were home now, come to think of it."

He started to rotate the ashtray again.

"Oh dear, don't tell me I'm making you nervous. We are nice, aren't we?"

"It's not a question of being nice, it's just—" He looked at me darkly.

"I was being outrageous. Forgive me."

He seemed greatly relieved.

"You are sweet," I said, not intending this for high praise.

"So are you."

"Oh no."

"But you are."

"No."

Our plates had been waiting for some time on the steely counter, under a pair of heat lamps whose red tinge made the food look radioactive. The waitress had been lost in thought—contemplating world affairs, it may be, or the perversity of Fate—but now she returned to the issues of the moment and carried us our omelettes. We dug in. Lucian had exquisite manners. I know because my mother branded the same into me. I'm sure he had learned them the way he had learned everything else: watching the right people—he had an instinct for finding these—do the right things.

We talked of Jules and my dinner with him. I told him all about Patty. Then Lucian asked me, with an assumption of cool disinterest, "What would you think of a man of forty who acts like a child? About personal matters, I mean. A very successful man and all, but who behaves like a teenager?"

"Hum," said I. "Sounds highly commendable. I like it."

"No you don't."

"Yes I do. Why do you ask?"

"Just tell me. You wouldn't act like a teenager, would you? Honestly."

"I might. With luck."

"Come on. You'd never be like this man, I'm telling you."

"This wouldn't happen to be your—"

"He's just a friend of mine."

"Not a friend of yours you live—"

"Just a friend, he's like a—"

"Jesus Christ, man, it's okay. He's your lover, yes? You live with him. Yes?"

He seemed astonished.

"Sweetheart, in this day and age your discretion is all but quaint. It's okay," I said, laughing.

He reached for my hand, which was idly tapping the frigid metal cream pitcher, and held me by the wrist for a moment. Then he asked, "Would you mind if I—"

I broke in without reflecting, "Do whatever you want. There are no rules between us. Those are the rules."

He stood, leaned across the table, and kissed my cheek. Tenderly. Sweetly. His mouth left a tingling spot that was conscious of itself for minutes, just at the top of my left cheekbone. He sat down.

We stared at each other.

What do I look like to him? I kept wondering. My eyes, like Jo's hair, are my only beauty. The rest of my face is comical and irregular, every Armour fault reverently handed down and duly suffered. Weak chins, dead white skin, narrow, crooked noses. In the worst cases Armours look as if at some crucial point in our development we were caught sideways in one of those murderous rooms whose walls close in to crush their helpless occupants (were there ever really such rooms?). Jules especially looks this way: shoulders hardly worthy of the distinction, just round places where the tops of the arms pin on—and what long lanky arms and legs, shapeless and gangling from adolescence to death. Iris at least had some hips and breasts; I am straight and narrow as the path of the righteous. Armours remind me of kitchen utensils, unlovely but handy. Except, as I say, for the eyes—but then, everyone's eyes are beautiful.

Whereas Lucian was perfect, the perfect man-boy. He had no self-consciousness about his beauty. He didn't need to have. He had no best angle to present, no weak profile to hide. It felt like a gift just to look at him—soft cheeks, straight nose, smooth wide forehead, thick, bright, curling hair. Radiant skin. Fine, mobile mouth. A cat may look at a king, I thought. Long, slender fingers. Proportion everywhere. There was more than formal perfection. His very presence suggested beauty, and an abundance of youth and pleasure, as if life itself lay strewn carelessly before and behind him, like flowers on a path. His gestures were easy, spontaneous, unerring. Where he kissed me his mouth had been soft and hot. Little escaped me. His eyes. Blue with a wash of violet.

My pain in looking at him was only that he had to look back at me. I wished I were beautiful, but I wasn't made for beauty. God gave Armours talent I guess and took away everything else. Well. God will have His little joke. Sometimes I felt downright sorry for Lucian, who traded the sight of my face for his.

FOUR

❧❦

I GAVE HIM DINNER that night and he told me about
his lover Ivory. To be honest I can't remember exactly how
it came about that I was to give him dinner. No doubt he
talked me into it. I think I said I'd make it for him but
since I had no pots or dishes I ended up sending out to a
Chinese place Jules recommended for two million little
paper drums and packets of rice and steaming vegetable
jumbles. I bought a few necessaries—candles, glasses. The
only thing I actually made was the table, which I built of
some loose bricks I found in the garden (every time I went
out there I heard Jules saying pointedly how impossible it
is to find such a garden in New York), just the right height
for sitting on the floor by, not quite symmetrical and not
quite otherwise, with a square recess inside it where I hid
a bottle of blackberry brandy—my sweetest and possibly
cheapest vice in those days. Oh yes, and I made a tape
(since I didn't have a stereo) of Chopin nocturnes, an hour
and a half of them, on my little cassette recorder, playing
on my newly arrived piano. I was rusty but enjoyed it, making ghastly errors and burying them under an excess of

romantic feeling that would embarrass Manilow. In the rawness of my situation these familiar pieces moved me unexpectedly.

If I do not have beauty I do have style. Dinner was a great success, a pleasant puzzle of forgotten boxes and impromptu implements, sort of a cross between a meal and a maze. Lucian was the most gratifying person to do things for I have ever met. This is not a gift to be scorned. We ate amid a cluster of narrow candles in tiny holders like stars. Lucian wore a biscuit-colored suit, which he'd explained on arrival (late, of course) as being necessary because of plans Ivory had made for that night. "We had a fight. I'm sorry. I couldn't get out of it. I'll have to leave at eleven."

"Not to worry."

"He's such a pain."

"Come in."

He took in the table, the candles, the tape. "This is wonderful," he said; and thereafter punctuated our conversation with this refrain every five minutes or so. He meant it, too— in fact, it seemed all he could do not to collapse of pure appreciation.

"Come sit down."

The table was near the long low back windows, in what was properly the dining room. We sat across from each other, I feeling awkward but merry, Lucian balance and ease itself. No matter how good and deserving I am, I notice, I never seem to become beautiful. This is a great distinction between real life and fairy tales. I caught a glimpse of myself in the dark back window and decided to devote my attention to dinner. "This thing tonight," Lucian was saying, "this thing Ivory committed us to, it's the opening

of a restaurant. It's the opening of this restaurant a friend
of his owns. All his friends are going."

I nabbed some bean sprouts with my chopsticks. "Oh.
Don't you like them?"

"Not much. We never see my friends. At this point I
hardly have any friends. Would you mind if I—"

"No rules," I said. "Whatever you want."

Lucian took his jacket and tie off and stretched out on
his side, leaning on one elbow.

"What's he do, your friend? Is that his first name, Ivory?"

"Martin. Martin Ivory. He's a film producer." He fought
a wild smile of pleasure at this exotic distinction belonging
to his lover, continuing as if in disgust, "He makes these
movies that are like—oh God, horror films, sci-fi. You
wouldn't like them. I don't like them. Sometimes they
don't even get released here. They make them for the foreign market."

"Do they now?"

"Yes," he said austerely. He knew I was laughing at him
but he didn't know why. It was the way he said "foreign
market." I could tell he'd just learned the phrase somewhere else. He used it with enjoyment. All through the
time I spent with him words I'd used would come back
at me like this—like exercises in a language class. Lucian
was learning a language. "Is there something humorous
about that?"

"Not a thing. So. What about your career?"

"I'm an actor. Didn't I tell you?"

"Haven't breathed a word of it."

"Well, I am."

"I kind of thought so."

"What does *that* mean?"

"Nothing, nothing. Less than nothing. Lucian, what about Ivory? Does he help you with your career?"

"That's the problem," he exploded. "No. Never, anything! It's such a small thing—it would be so easy for him; but I think he's afraid if I make a living I'll leave him. He won't help me get an agent. I was trying to see one yesterday in fact, when I saw you. He's so crazy on the subject I can't even talk to him about it—but I've got to get an agent. You can't get work if you don't have an agent."

"I see."

"All I ever do now is take acting classes. Ivory pays for those, I have to say that. But I hardly ever get to class, you know, he drags me to so many screenings and tapings and locations and openings . . . Jesus. You have to work at acting."

"Do you?"

"Well hell yes."

I chased a water chestnut around for a while, then skewered it in a fit of pique. "That must be frustrating for you," I mumbled, crunching it.

"Well, it is. Ivory thinks acting's just talking in front of the camera. You should hear the way he talks about actors, like they were animals or something, Jesus. He doesn't think I need to go to classes. He doesn't understand anything about serious acting."

"Are you a serious actor?"

"Yes." He looked at me in mild surprise. "Aren't you a serious songwriter?"

"Hardly."

"You take pride in your craft, don't you? You try to perfect it, right? I mean, you don't just put down anything that comes into your head at the keyboard."

"No—but then I can't do that. It wouldn't make a good song."

"That's what I mean. Ivory thinks you just put down whatever comes into your head. That's his idea of art; he knows absolutely nothing. He treats writers almost as badly as he treats actors. He thinks we're idiots because we don't make money. I mean, because that's not the main thing we do."

"That's the main thing I do," I said.

"It is? No it's not."

"Have some rice," I said.

"It isn't," he pursued. "Your songs are really good."

"Thank you."

"No, don't say thank you. I'm not complimenting you, I'm saying I think you can really write."

I blinked at him.

"I expect great things of you."

"But Lucian, why?" I laughed.

"Because, you have talent. I can feel it. And you have guts."

"Is that a fact?"

"Yes. You can be a great artist."

"Sweetheart, you need more than that," I said.

"Like what?"

"Like, I don't know—the desire to be one. I don't know."

"You'll do it."

"I see. This is very interesting. So then, you too are planning to be a great artist I presume?"

"You can laugh at me all you want, I'm telling you this is going to happen."

"I'm listening," I said. "Go ahead and take the last egg roll. Tell me why you're in love with Ivory."

"I don't know if I'm in love with Ivory. I mean I am, but . . . He doesn't believe in art at all. He doesn't believe in anything, really. We practically never see a play unless a friend of his produced it or something."

"Can't you go alone?"

"Ivory likes me to stay near him."

"Oh?"

"He likes to show me off. You're sure you don't want this?"

"Positive."

He took the egg roll with delicate fingers. "Ivory likes to show me off I think. We're never alone."

"You must love him a little or you wouldn't be with him."

"Maybe. I guess. He loves me, anyway. We just have this—kind of stormy relationship, I don't know. We live a very complicated life."

"I see." I retired my chopsticks and poured out some brandy, some for Lucian, some for me.

"Sometimes I think I can't stand it anymore. I'm not happy with him."

"I know. "

"I'm telling you more than I've told anyone."

"I know."

"I don't trust too many people."

"Neither do I."

He watched me carefully. "Sometimes I think I'll run away," he said.

I waited.

"Once I did. I have this friend named Jeannie in Boston. You'd like Jeannie."

"I doubt that."

"You would. I stayed there five days, almost. Ivory never knew where I was. He called Jeannie but she lied for me. When I came back he was practically crazy."

"That was crummy of you," I said.

"You should see the stuff he's done to me." He paused, looking down at a candle, then up at me again.

"If you run away to me," I said, "I won't lie for you. You'll have to tell Ivory just where you are."

"I've thought of that."

"I know you have."

"Of running away to you, I mean."

"I know."

"I'm not happy there."

"I know."

We watched each other over the candles and the table. The wash of violet in Lucian's eyes was soft, like a veil or a mist.

"You'd better go," I said.

"Okay."

"You don't want to be late."

"No, I guess not." Meditatively he took a sip of brandy. "It's peaceful here."

I smiled.

"We have a lot to give each other."

"Maybe," I said. Lucian stood up and put on his tie and jacket. I followed him to the door.

"This was perfect," he said.

"Thanks for coming."

He kissed me full on the mouth, startling me, his mouth warm and fragrant with blackberry brandy and plum sauce. I felt oddly moved, as if someone had impulsively told me a secret. I wondered what, if anything, it meant to him.

FIVE

※

THE NEXT FIVE DAYS were devoted to lunacy. I was supposed to be writing Tommy Enright's song, but the minute I sat down to do it the phone would ring and there would be Lucian suggesting a cheerful and usually frivolous expedition to which I would invariably agree within a few minutes. Chief among these was the trip we made to the zoo, which started humbly as a proposed jaunt through Central Park and ended up an elaborate spin alongside the Hudson, taking·in the Bronx Zoo and the Botanical Gardens on the way and finally involving an inn near Ossining. Lucian never had money, not even cab fare, and everything he touched turned to expense. However, he was a gifted taker, as I have mentioned, and it was long long long before I minded.

I realized what Lucian wanted most now was an agent. I don't know why, but I assumed he was not a good actor. Something about his earnestness maybe. Nevertheless an agent was what he wanted, so I started thinking about agents. In a quiet moment while avoiding work I phoned Jules one day at the *Beat*. Behind his voice was what sounded like the Busy Office sound effects tape from a radio drama—very impressive. A little nervously I launched into my request, beginning with, "I have a friend, he's an actor, and he needs—"

"An agent," Jules finished.

"How'd you know?"

"Everyone needs an agent."

"Oh." I didn't like his tone of voice. I worked the curly phone cord through my fingers like a secular rosary. "Could you help him, do you think?"

"Have him make an audition tape. He leaves it with the agent, they review it—that's the best way. Okay?"

"What kind of tape?"

Jules mustered his best Armour-explains-quantum-theory-to-a-moron voice. "A videotape. Four or five minutes of monologue, maybe two monologues, one classical, one contemporary. He'll know what I mean if he's an actor. Everyone does them. Does he have any money?"

"Oh yes. Sure," I said promptly.

"Then there's no problem. Just tell him to call a commercial videotape place and have himself filmed."

"And then?"

"And then nothing. What do you mean?"

"I mean, what does he do with it once he's got it?"

"He takes it around to agents, I told you."

"Will they look at it Jules?" I worked the rosary backwards.

"Yeah they'll look—well no, maybe not. It depends how lucky he is."

"Well I don't know how lucky he is, so do you know any agents, Jules?"

"Who is this guy to you?"

"Jules, I don't like to ask you, but would you arrange to

have it looked at for him? You must know someone."

"What kind of work does he want?" he asked, in the patented Armour-gets-his-hand-tacked-to-a-cross voice.

"Theatrical, I think."

"But he'll take what he can get, I presume?"

"I'm not sure." I doubled the phone cord back across my knuckles and looped it over my thumb.

"How old is he?"

"Seventeen."

"Jesus, Melanie, who is this guy to you? What does he want to play, juveniles?"

"I don't know, Jules."

"Yeah, well if he's seventeen and he's going to you for favors he'll take what he can get. Just have him make the tape." He sighed. "Then call me."

"Thank you. God will reward you for this."

"That's what I'm afraid of."

I told Lucian all about this the day we went up to the inn on the Hudson. I waited till dessert. The dining room was large, full of heavy white napery with pressed edges shiny from years of use, and staffed by uncomplaining middle-aged waiters who looked somehow like a phalanx of uncles. At first he was very excited; then, "Oh, but it must cost a lot. I can't afford it."

"I'll cover it."

"No, you can't—"

"Yes I can."

"Well then, I can't—"

"Just take it. You'll pay me back."

"I would, you know," he said.

"I know. It's no trouble for me."

He looked at me in silence a moment. "You realize Ivory

would never arrange for something like that because it might take me out of his control," he said. "You're so wonderful."

"Don't be ridiculous."

He stood and walked around the table, kissed me on the forehead, then walked back calmly to his place and sat down again. "I love you," Lucian said feelingly.

I didn't answer.

"Now," he went on unconcernedly when a minute or two had gone by. "Where should we stop on the way home?"

⚘

One night Lucian slept with me. He'd gone out to Southampton with Ivory for the weekend, but on Sunday afternoon he showed up on my doorstep, tired and miserable, saying he shouldn't have gone. "It's too crazy, those people out there. I left, I just took off."

"Who are they?"

He wandered in toward the kitchen. "You wouldn't have any of that blackberry brandy left would you?" he asked. "God, that would taste so good." He sat down, exhausted, in the doorway to the kitchen. I still had no furniture. I poured him a glass. "It's so hot out. Did I disturb you?" He glanced out at the piano.

"No."

"We had the most awful argument. I got absolutely no sleep last night, none." He held onto his forehead. "Ivory has these guys staying out there for the weekend, you know? He's trying to be real chummy with them so he can get permission to do some location shooting where they come from, for some horror film—I don't know. They're from this Central American country, you know, El something or San something, and one of them's on the filmboard—Jesus, Melanie, I don't know. The point is Ivory wants something from them so he invited them to spend the weekend. He does this all the time."

"Does what?"

"Invites people. Bribes them. Do you think that's wrong? He's bribed judges. Everyone owes him a favor."

"I think that's how some people run their businesses."

"That's how he runs his. You wouldn't believe it. And naturally I'm supposed to be extra friendly to whoever he's interested in."

"I see."

He leaned his curly head on the door frame, closing his eyes. He looked frail and very beautiful. "You live so nicely," he said, after a silence. "Do you think I could stay here tonight?"

"I think so."

"I don't want to go home."

"Then don't."

"I could but I don't want to be there when Ivory gets back. He'll still have all those people with him. All those people. God." He opened his eyes. "You know I think Ivory's afraid to be alone."

"Who isn't?"

"No, I mean really afraid."

"So do I."

"You aren't afraid," he said.

"That's what you think."

"You're alone," he pointed out.

"That's only because I'm just as afraid of being with someone."

41

"I don't believe you."

So we slept together that night. Besides the piano, Daphne's old bed was the only furniture in the house. After dinner I made Lucian call Ivory's exchange and leave a message saying where he was. I still had a lot to do on my song so I sat at the piano and tried to work while Lucian considered monologues down in the garden. The heat—that famous New York humid heat—had continued to poison the days, but the air conditioner had proved effective and the night was solace itself. If it weren't for ants and madmen I might have slept in the garden. I didn't get much accomplished that evening. Lucian interrupted me about twelve times, finally to say he was going to bed. "Aren't you coming?" he asked. "It's one already."

I sat on the piano bench, tapping my pencil on the edge of middle C and watching him, my eyes I think opaque. He hovered awkwardly at the top of the stairs. "No, you go ahead," I said at last.

"You come too. It'll be nice to fall asleep together."

I stood and followed him, turning out lights. He went out into the garden again to look at the stars while I washed up, pulled on an oversized Eagles T-shirt, and climbed into bed. I called him in. I'd bought new sheets and pillows. The sheets had the scratchy feel sheets do when you haven't ever washed them, and the pillows were too full and stiff. I lay on my back, my hands joined beneath my head. Behind me I heard Lucian running the tap. I looked, unseeing, into the garden.

"You can use my toothbrush," I called over the sound of the water.

"Already did."

I smiled. In a few minutes Lucian came into the room,

still in his shirt, his legs and feet bare. He climbed into the bed and curled up against me. I turned the lamp off with one arm and put the other around him. A bright even coat of blue moonlight painted the sliding glass door.

"Good-night," said Lucian, kissing my cheek.

"Good-night." He lay still by my side. "You don't kick, do you?" I said.

"Kick? I don't think so."

"Iris kicked. My sister."

"Oh."

I looked at the top of his head as if I could see through it.

"How did she die?"

"She walked across a street."

"What?"

"And a car hit her. Accident. She died immediately."

"Oh. God." I felt his breath through my T-shirt, on my shoulder; his head lay heavily against me. I wished I felt sleepier. "How old were you then?"

"Twenty-two. Iris was twenty-nine." I realized it for the first time. "I'm older than that now."

"Are you?"

"Thirty. God, she'd been married for years by then. She had a four-year-old daughter."

"Megan, right?"

"Right."

"What happened to her husband?"

"Nothing. What do you mean?"

"Donald, isn't it? How did he take it? Did it—shatter him?"

I wondered where he had heard that deaths shatter people. "No. He was shaken I guess, but he's—well I told you, he's kind of pure and saintly. He just kept going. He left NYU and moved up to Maine with my mother. He teaches at a little college up there now. He sort of handed Megan over to my mother to raise, you know, but other than that— life just went on."

"Did he love her?"

"I think so. Who knows? You can't see into a marriage like that."

"Do you miss her?"

"Yes;" and suddenly, lying with Lucian in my arms, I did miss Iris terribly. A picture of her burst into my brain like a bullet: I saw her putting sheets in a drawer in the house we grew up in together. Sunlight fell across her bent back and seeped through her thin blue Ship 'n' Shore blouse. The narrow waistband of her cotton skirt buckled slightly, just over her spine. She'd made the skirt herself: I could see where she'd put the zipper in wrong. As she settled the sheets at the back of the drawer she turned to look at me. I saw her clear Armour eyes and her mouse-brown hair lit up from behind, electric wisps flying from a meager French knot. Then the image retired to take its place in my file of images of her.

"I guess you don't really get over something like that," Lucian said from the imperfect darkness.

"I guess not." Before I knew what it was a tear was on my cheek, mine. I wanted to hide it before Lucian divined its presence. I brushed it away. I hardened myself to drive off the sadness. "Good-night," I said.

"Are you all right?"

"I'm fine."

"Good-night then." He kissed me. I thought of Iris, how she used to tell me to sleep in her bed if our parents were out, or when I got scared. One summer she'd pasted her bedroom ceiling with a thick nebula of fluorescent stars she ordered from the back of an Archy comic book. All night long they gave off gently the light they absorbed each day. I was so much younger than she that for years I believed her ceiling was magical. I suspected Iris of some clandestine trafficking with the spirit of Night, or with God Himself. My parents sold that house a long time ago.

Lucian was falling asleep beside me. In the moonlit dark his soft cheeks glowed as Iris's stars had done. After a while he turned on his stomach. He slept with his arms flung over his head, his profile as clear and bright against the sheets as the head on a Mercury dime. I sleep on my belly too, but I tuck my hands underneath me, just where my hips and legs come together. I haven't figured out yet whether this is to protect my hands from the world while I sleep or, less plausible but I think more likely, to protect the world from my hands.

ᙾ

I woke up long before Lucian, no great feat since he slept till noon. I've never been much of a lingerer in beds but I did pause a few minutes that morning to watch him, to listen to his shallow, airy breathing, just generally to take advantage of my first good unhurried look at him. He'd taken his shirt off during the night. I could see the fine blond down on his shoulders and back where the morning poured in across him. His vertebrae had an extreme, unexpected spikiness: they rose like a string of tiny atolls down the long reef of spine. I got up and washed at the kitchen sink so as not to disturb him. Daphne's ominous report notwithstanding I never heard the pipes make noise in that place.

Lucian woke up finally and wandered upstairs with a lot

45

of eye-rubbing and it's-not-really-twelve-is-it, and did I mind
if he took a shower and God Ivory would kill him.

"Why?"

"I, um . . . I took his Jag when I left Southampton. I
wonder how he and the rest of them got home."

"You're kidding."

"I wish," he said with feeling.

"Lucian, you jerk, you left him stranded?"

"Not exactly stranded. He has a limo; he probably sent
his driver back to the city to get it." He ambled curiously
over to the piano, where I was crossing out words. I was
glad he was up. It isn't easy for me to work silently and today was my last day to get the song done. I had to pack,
too.

"I leave for Maine tomorrow, you know," I said.

"I know. It's horrible."

"Come have dinner with me tonight, okay?"

He sat down by me on the piano bench, experimentally
shaping a G major chord. "Could we have lunch or something? Ivory's going to be furious."

"Nope. Sorry. I'm having lunch with Jules, at one. In
fact you better get going."

"Shit."

"We could skip it. Say good-bye now—"

"No, no, I want to see you. Shit. I'll just have to put
Ivory off. Let me go home now and talk to him."

"Okay."

"I'll be back around eight, okay?" He stood up.

"Are you sure?"

"Yes."

"I don't want you to leave and then find out it was the
last time we got to see each other after all."

"God Melanie, don't you think we'll see each other? After August I mean?"

"Life is full of surprises."

"You *better* see me."

"Go take your shower."

"Melanie—"

"Of course I'll see you. I'll see you. I just wonder what you'll be like by then."

"God." He disappeared, muttering, down the stairs.

If you count nine as being 'around eight,' Lucian was on time that night. We ate at a local crêperie, though I hated eating with him in the Village. There were always so many gay men there, so many looks flying back and forth around him. He never seemed to notice, but I did.

"Lucian," I asked as the unnaturally attentive waiter brought us our coffee, "what does Ivory make of me?"

"What?"

"What does he think our relationship is? Does he know who I am?" I pushed the cream over to him.

"What do you mean, who you are? You mean, does he know your work?" he asked. "Yes." Besides cream, Lucian took three lumps of sugar in his coffee. I don't think he really liked coffee at all; he just thought it made him seem grown up to drink it.

"No, I mean to you. Does he know who I am to you."

"He knows you're my friend."

"Oh. Well, I guess that's right."

"Of course that's right. What do you mean?"

"Nothing. I thought he might find me a threat."

"Why should he? Aren't you my friend?"

"Yes I am."

"Well good. Because I need to ask you a favor."

47

"Oh boy." I deliberately spilled water on the red-checked oilcloth, then tried to float bits of crust across the resulting puddle. Most of them sank.

"First tell me if you finished your song."

"Yes. And thanks for all your concern."

"Did it come out well?"

"I think so." Actually it had come out much better than I'd expected, I couldn't have said why at the time, especially with all the running around Lucian and I had been doing.

"That's great. I was wondering in that case if maybe you'd help me with my audition tape."

"Oh God."

"I went to the theater library today, at Lincoln Center, but I couldn't find anything I wanted to do. Everybody does the same pieces over and over, you know. I was thinking it would be really neat if I sort of wrote something myself. I want to. What do you think, will you help me?"

"Oh Lucian. I hate collaborating."

"You wouldn't have to do much. I'd do the real work. You'd be like—an adviser."

"I bet."

"You would. It'd be so good for me. It only has to last a few minutes. Anyway, it'd be wonderful working together. We bring out the best in each other."

"I used to have to collaborate at Helicon, in the early days. They'd set it up . . . ugh, it was awful. Anyhow, I'm going away."

"But this would be me you'd be working with. I've got it all figured out. We could do it in the mail, or maybe you'd come down to New York some time—"

"Can't."

"Or maybe I could come up. If you invited me," he added politely.

"Maybe," I said. I abandoned my puddle and, wetting a finger, distractedly tried to raise a hum from the rim of my water glass.

"Then you'll help me? Please, it would be so wonderful."

"I know nothing about drama."

"You don't have to. I do. You're good with words, you can do it. Please? Maybe you could even write some music for the—"

"No."

The barrage suddenly ceased. Then, "You think I'm a jerk, don't you? You don't want to work with me." He looked as if he might be about to stand up.

"No of course not. Wait. Sit down. I mean—"

He looked at me hopefully.

"Okay, okay, you're on. But you're going to do all the writing, okay? I edit. That's all."

"Right. That's all. Oh Melanie, you're an angel." He swallowed the last of his syrupy coffee. "Let's get the hell out of here."

We emerged from the restaurant into the cooling street. I could not get used to the smell of the streets in New York. It seemed to me it was to tar and filth what earthiness is to earth. Lucian put his arm around me as we walked home and told me his thoughts for the monologue so far. He thought it would be neat to show a guy who had to make a decision—a young guy maybe who was stuck between a man and a woman.

"This woman is older than he is, you know? But maybe he's sort of in debt to the man. The man is older than he is too, and it's like he's a powerful . . . lawyer or something.

Or maybe a director. Maybe the young guy's an actor, see, and he's met this woman by chance or something—it doesn't matter how—and even though he's in love with this man—he's gay, the actor or whatever he is, he feels this kind of kinship to the woman," he explained excitedly. This baffling scenario, based on I couldn't imagine whose life, was expounded to me in glorious detail and at quite some substantial length. At first I laughed at it, thinking Lucian must see the humor too, but true to form, he didn't. He never considered anything to do with himself funny. I settled down and tried to take him seriously. When we got home we went down into the garden to lie on our backs on the patio a while and look at the stars and the fireflies.

"I'll just mail you whatever I have whenever I can," said Lucian, still excited. "You can write back your ideas when you have a chance, okay?"

"Okay."

"You don't have to worry about answering right away."

"Thanks."

"Only try to answer as soon as you can, will you?"

I laughed. "Okay." Something told me Lucian was not going to get around to working on this while I was gone anyway. I wondered what our relationship would be by the time I got back, if anything. The likelihood of its collapsing had distracted me all day. "Remind me to give you my address," I said.

"Do you really think you won't be down till September?"

"I'm sure I won't. Besides everything else, I have a feeling my mother may be sick again. I don't want to leave her alone if she is."

"Is she sick a lot?"

"Mm-huh."

"Your family doesn't have very good luck," he observed.

"Not very." The bricks were crumbly and uneven beneath us but they still retained some of the day's heat. A warm wind dusted the garden. "My mother's a special case though. She's very secretive about these things. Her health is never really great. She drives me nuts," I remarked.

"Maybe I'll meet her."

"Maybe."

"Is it beautiful up there? It must be."

"Very."

"God that would be wonderful."

"You don't really think Ivory would let you go?" I asked.

He didn't answer for a minute. Then, "Ivory doesn't own me," he said.

"Hmm. Well if you can come, you're welcome."

"Anyway, I'll call," he said thickly.

"I don't want you to run up a lot of calls to me on Ivory's bill, please."

"He wouldn't even notice. You should see his phone bill."

"That's not my point."

"Sometimes I think I might do some modeling and make a little money of my own," Lucian said. "This agency, it's a really good agency, said they would take me on if I wanted. It's a really good agency," he repeated.

"I don't doubt it."

"Only Ivory thinks it's stupid."

"Listen Lucian," I blurted out, "I want you to keep a key to my place. Will you do that?"

"What?"

"What if yesterday happens again, if you need a place to run and I'm not around? I don't like you being so dependent on Ivory. At least take the key in case, okay?"

"Are you sure?"

"Of course. I won't even be here."

"Oh Melanie." He propped himself up on one elbow and looked down at me through the moonlight. There was a floodlight of course but I hadn't turned it on. I hate electric lighting out of doors. "You're an angel."

"Don't be silly."

He continued to look at me steadily. "I don't think I've ever had a friend like you," he said. "Wait a minute." He jumped up, full of energy all of the sudden, and tore through the garden to the back wall.

"What are you doing?"

"Just a minute." I heard a rustle as he broke something off. There were flowers and bushes all over the back wall, and vines that trailed in from the neighbors'.

"Well, what is it?" I asked, getting up on my elbow too. Crickets kept time in the dark garden. The wind was fragrant and soft.

"Just be patient. Lie down again." He came back to me. "Open your mouth. Close your eyes."

"What are you doing?"

"Just open." He kneeled beside me, a flowery something in his hand. "Melanie—"

"What, what?"

"Melanie, close your eyes. Open your mouth." He added exasperatedly, "I'm not going to hurt you."

I did as he told me. In an instant a delicious droplet swam on my tongue, cool, absolutely sweet, hardly more substantial than a snowflake. I rose to my elbow again.

"No, let me do it over," said Lucian, immensely pleased with himself.

"What are you doing?" I demanded.

"Just keep your eyes shut. Lie down."

"Lucian, what is it?"

"Shut up—"

"What *is* it?"

"It's honeysuckle," he finally said, laughing with pleasure. "Don't you know? You pull the stem out backwards and there's a drop of nectar in each flower. Wait, close your eyes and I'll do it again."

"No." I sat up completely, pained and astonished at my own ignorance. "No, I don't know. Show me." All these years and no one had ever told me this secret before. My eyes filled with tears before I could stop them, not only from sadness but from shame and anger too. Why was I never told about this? We had a trellis of honeysuckle at home in Sands Point, now I came to think of it. Lucian was laughing at me with delight. He twisted some honeysuckle flowers into my hair.

SIX

❧

TO ARRIVE AT Milk Lake Farm, near Webster, Maine, one begins by arriving at Augusta. To arrive at Augusta one takes a commuter plane from Boston. Boston one reaches on one's own. From Augusta there's the bus to Bruton, and from Bruton one makes shift. My mother was to have picked me up but at the last minute found she couldn't. She was sorry, she explained, in a voice that suggested I actively supposed she was not. Things had just been—too hectic, too chaotic. I'd be all right. Would I? Yes. Thank you. It had nothing to do with not being glad to see me, naturally. No, naturally not. She couldn't wait to see me, as a matter of fact. So I would just call the cab in Bruton, okay? Okay. It was nothing. And anyway, she pointed out, we'd have a whole month together at the Farm.

Lucian was supposed to have gone with me to La Guardia but at the last minute (there was a lot of this going around that morning) it seemed that Ivory needed him. He just managed to nip down, take the key and say good-bye again. I asked him to have a duplicate made and send it to me in Maine. Jules had a second key to my place but somehow I didn't feel like explaining to him how and why this young person might be needing it. I had to stop up at Helicon on my way out to the airport—suitcases and all—to leave this famous song Patty awaited so anxiously. I felt kind of strange in the elevator on the way down. It happened to be the same car where I had first seen Lucian a week before.

In truth, in very truth, I wasn't at all crazy about leaving New York just then. Besides being curious about Lucian Curry, I had hardly had time to get my adventuring started. I didn't want the city to get the idea I had given up. I was going to live there if it killed me. Moreover, the prospect of being in a place where only owls and bats have a nightlife scared me half to pieces. I'm not used to being on my own all night. I like plenty of company in the dark.

Yet, it gratified me deeply to have been asked by my mother to visit. She had so little use for me as a rule. Now, even if her request had been made only to suit herself, I had something to give her. That was rare and pleasant. And I looked forward to seeing her again. I imagined it would be interesting to view her with what I flattered myself was a wiser, more independent vision. Besides, I wanted to find out how much of Iris had shown up in Megan so far. I love my family, God help me. All of them. Awkward, awkward, awkward for an Armour. I was curious too about Sharon Dennison, who had, it appeared, managed to startle Donald out of his waking dream. I even wanted to see the Farm itself. I hadn't been there in years.

There's something so sweet and pathetic about La Guardia Airport. You know no one there can be going anywhere particular. Even the newsstands have an apologetic look, like they maybe belong in the Port Authority. All the travelers seem tinged with hopelessness, except the tiniest children and some of the businessmen. Everyone knows that everyone knows we're not going anyplace really. Nothing is entirely clean. The artificial light just misses the glare and glamour of bigtime terminals. Airlines cling touchingly to the protocol, the uniforms, the formality of international carriers. Loudspeakers blare to half a dozen people what gate they should go to. The gate turns out to be just gray metal doors where you walk out onto the airfield. Logan in Boston is the same but more so, if you're on your way up to Augusta. The commuter planes are so small you can't stand up in them, and the wind currents push them around however they jolly well please. The pilot and stewardess merge into one semi-uniformed ordinary person. Pretense is left behind. The airport in Augusta is about the size of a good Dairy Queen in New Jersey.

The heat in Maine was painful but uniform, as if controlled by an impoverished yet beneficent government that, though it couldn't come up with the price of a breeze, was at least determined to make its citizens share equally in the awful visitation of sun. Enough has been said, I think, about buses, and how pleasant they are. Boarding for Bruton, I heard an elderly Englishwoman ahead of me telling the driver she'd kill him if anything happened to her luggage. He wouldn't let her keep it with her. He put it in that compartment under the seats that opens from the side of the bus. He shoved my things in after hers while she stood watching in the hot sun, again threatening death if anything broke or disappeared. "Fifty bucks in it for you if you lose mine," I murmured. Nobody laughed. I was in Maine.

The anxious English lady sat next to me. I left her still fretting when I got off. I called Webster Cabs Incorporated, and they sent their consumptive fleet of one to take me the rest of the way. The driver was Bobby Axelrod, who French-kissed me one summer at a Bruton Junior Boosters dance. He didn't recognize me till he saw where we were going. I overtipped him. It wasn't exactly Harry Chapin.

Then I was home, because say what you like, home is wherever you have to keep going back to. I arrived about five. The afternoon sun made sharp black shadows of the trees on the long gray driveway. I walked up over them, a suitcase in either hand, feeling obscurely as if each step incriminated me in some phantom crime. The huge rambly farmhouse had been painted a new shade of slate blue since I'd last seen it. The place seemed less rural now than ever. I realized suddenly there was gravel on the drive. It had always been scraped dirt. Mother had been improving things. With a presentiment of catastrophe that had nothing to do with psychic phenomena I lifted the big brass knocker, held it a moment, then let it fall. You might as well just not leave, as far as the folks at home are concerned. They take up with you right where they left off.

Megan answered the door, wearing starchy-looking jeans and a clean T-shirt. Her hair was in terrifyingly symmetrical pigtails. She was almost twelve now, taller, and less pretty, alas. The last time I'd seen her she looked like Donald. Now the fatal Armour traits were surfacing. She was going to resemble me, poor thing. I trembled for her adolescence.

She kissed me decorously. "Grandma's upstairs," she said. She was excruciatingly demure, distinctly my mother's victim. "On the phone."

Of course. "Well let's go," I said. I followed her through the shadowy front hall. I was almost as surprised to see the old familiar knickknacks and pictures and plants as if they'd been moon rocks and arctic debris. They've been living here all this while, I kept realizing. The house felt the wrong size. I was sure the doorway to the dining room had been a little higher, the living room a bit farther back. The illusion vanished by the time I'd gone upstairs and come down again, but for the moment it was vivid. I was curious to see the rest of the place again. The trick of the Armour home-coming is the subtle way you participate in your own demise. Like climbing up to the gallows. You put yourself out a little to meet your fate. Megan ahead of me, I ascended the wooden stairs to my mother. Two at a time, in fact. What the h dash double l.

I was about to say my mother was just as I'd remembered her, but it's truer to say she was just as I'd forgotten her. She had hardly changed, except to age two years, her face more crumpled and white under the pink veil of powder she always wore. For an instant I thought, There's an old woman in my mother's bedroom. Then I recognized her. She was Mother, whose vigilant eyes had met mine through a hundred mostly nasty emotions, who had had to look down to see me once upon a time and now always had to look up. Old love, aching and thick, rose in my throat like a fever. I wanted to fuse my life with hers, make her young again with my youth. I wanted to keep her by me forever. Tears stung my eyes. I must certainly outlive her. Then it was all swept away by her smile, the wide, pleasant smile she always put on to look gladder than she was to see me. Anger rose up where the love had been. A riptide of despair pulled me out toward a dangerous sea.

"Melanie!"

"Mother."

She spoke to the phone. "Jules, Melanie's just come in. I'd better go." Hand over the phone. "Just a minute Melanie. Jules, think about it. Only if you want to. I thought it would be nice for you. Yes." There was a pause. I waited in the doorway, clumsy and superfluous. "No, just a minute. There was something else . . . No, it's gone now. Well, can we finish this later? I really must go dear. Yes." She dropped the receiver into its cradle and held out her arms to me. She didn't stand up though. I went to her chair. We embraced.

Her room was the same, an extremely civilized room with wide banks of white-latticed windows on three walls and two shiny painted doors flanking the fourth. On that fourth wall was the bed, an expansive white affair frothy with eyelet and ribbons and gauze. My mother's bed had been white ever since I could remember. A profusion of roses splashed across the crisp wallpaper and was repeated everywhere—on the draperies, on the porcelain doorknobs, in the color of the carpet and the shade of lipstick on my mother's mouth. A bouquet of real roses stood near her, cut from the garden that morning no doubt and now dying slowly in a crystal vase. It was a room of generic prettiness. I wondered how my father had endured it; but perhaps it didn't matter to him. We didn't see much of my father when I was growing up—at least I didn't. I have a photograph of my parents on their wedding day. My mother wears a full-skirted lace-draped gown suspiciously like what later became their bed. My father holds her hand and stands a little behind her, the light from the camera's flash making his glasses bright and partially erasing his eyes. He looks, not to put too fine a point on it, like the fall guy in a con job: eager, average, and doomed.

My mother was seated in a low, squarish armchair, the

same she had sat in all through my childhood. There was no other chair in the room, but she waved me to the rose-bespattered ottoman. Megan lay on her stomach on the bed.

"Jules says hello," my mother told Megan.

"Hello back," said Megan.

"He seems edgy. I suggested he come up here for a weekend some time. Melanie, this is so lovely, having you here. I want to hear all about leaving L.A. and your new apartment and—how is your new apartment, is it lovely?"

"It's fine. It's—"

"Wasn't that fortunate, Jules's friend moving out just when you needed a place?"

"Yes, though actually I could have come east earlier."

"What exactly happened with you and that drummer—Michael, I think it was?" she asked suddenly, her voice soggy with solicitousness.

"Well I think I told you he—"

"Would you rather wait?" She glanced at Megan. "Tell me about your music first. Are you still with Helicon?"

"I've got to figure that out. My contract comes up for re-negotiation in October. If I sign it I commit myself to writing the same—"

"Megan, your shoes are on the bed. Excuse me dear, what were you saying?"

"Just that—"

"You should have seen Megan yesterday. She was our hero. Our heroine, I should say. The SAAB wouldn't start, when I had to take Donald to the airport. Just when I'd given up and gone inside to call the taxi, Megan—what did you do exactly, dear?"

"I fixed it."

"No, but what did you do? She was really something.

You'd have been proud of her. Tell Aunt Melanie what you did."

"That's okay," said Megan, looking at her hands.

"She—what do you call that?"

"I replaced the fuse to the starter." Megan stared down at the bedspread and played with a piece of lacy fringe. "That's all."

"I don't know where children learn these things."

"In school," Megan said, almost inaudibly.

"They're so clever. Can you imagine a little girl knowing so much about cars? Donald doesn't. I certainly don't. I really think the sexual revolution has succeeded." She shook her head at Megan to indicate amazement and admiration. "Come give Grandma a kiss."

Megan obediently rolled off the bed and trotted stiffly to her. She kissed her powdery cheek, then stood uncertainly by her side. I wondered how my mother must look to her—ancient, I suppose.

"Mmm," said my mother, squeezing Megan, who remained stiff and stared at me. "I love you. Now. Melanie, do you want to freshen up before dinner? You must be exhausted."

"Daddy said to say Hello, Melanie," Megan suddenly volunteered.

"Oh yes, about Donald," I began, but my mother interrupted me.

"Let's discuss that later," she said, with another look askance at Megan.

"Well I only wanted to say—"

"Ooooh Melanie, it's so good to see you," my mother squealed in a sad falsetto she sometimes used. "Sharon's made the most delicious chicken—"

"Where is Sharon?"

"Just delicious, you can smell it, and there's grapefruit to start with . . . The grapefruit's been out of this world lately, have you had any? Luscious. We live on it. Why don't you go on and get yourself settled while Megan and I go downstairs?"

"I want to help Melanie."

"Sweetheart, I need you to help me. We'll just let Aunt Melanie see to her own things." She had stood up and was patting down the skirt of her flowered shirtwaist. I was surprised to see how thin she had grown. Though she had always been trim she was now almost gaunt.

"Mother, are you all right? You don't look well."

"I'm fine Melanie, fine." She turned away from me. You could still use her back for a plumb line. She held out a hand for Megan, who took it reluctantly. The two of them crossed to the door.

"I don't know why I shouldn't look well," my mother murmured, apparently affronted. "Can you manage your suitcases? Dinner will be ready in half an hour. It's early because Sharon has to go home."

"All right."

"And then I want to hear all about New York." She left with Megan in tow. I listened to them descending the stairs, my mother telling Megan to call me Aunt Melanie, not Melanie.

I stood up feeling slightly killed and went down the long hall to my room. Megan lived in Iris's old room, Donald in Jules's. Mine was intact still, and though most of my childhood and high school things had been packed (or thrown) away when my parents moved up from Sands Point, this room was filled with summer mementos. There was my rock and feather collection, small rounded stones from the lake mostly, stacks of programs from summer concerts in Bruton and Augusta, two tennis racquets minus the strings, old white Keds with the soles warped and cracked from walking in the lake in them, a cameo-backed mirror that used to be Iris's, two sketches she did of the Farm, the set of Sir Walter Scott I read when I was twelve, boxes of unused psychedelic stationery, bundles of summer letters from Sands Point friends. The room was a small one but I'd always liked it. It had blue and white curtains and a marine-blue carpet and an alcove with a window seat of dark varnished wood that opened to reveal a recess below it. The bed was a twin. I'd forgotten that. It swayed and squeaked alarmingly when I first sat on it, as if to protest that it hadn't been expecting anyone. It had a pine headboard I'd once scratched my name on in pen, I don't know why. My mother had had it sanded away.

It was good to be alone for a minute. I wondered, though, how come my mother had spirited Megan off so pointedly. I found out later that she had a reason, to wit, to keep me from spilling the beans about Donald and Sharon. I was always finding out later that she had a reason. My half-hour's grace was soon ended. I descended to the dining room, the only ugly room in the house. No matter what was done to it it remained steadfast in its ugliness. It held to it as to a solemn duty.

At dinner things went from unpromising to terrible. From the moment I took my place at the table; at the mere sound of my mother's changeless Good Evening Melanie; at the very sight of her silver grapefruit spoon held aloft, its cruel teeth about to dive into the tender fruit, her pink fingers curled and poised around its handle like a tiny, aging corps de ballet, merciless, vicious, pure contrariness gripped me as if we had never been parted.

"Hello," I said, tossing my napkin, still folded, into my lap.

"Good evening, Aunt Melanie."

"You don't have to call me aunt."

Megan looked at her grandmother.

"You are her aunt."

"Yes, but there's no point in insisting on it. It sounds ridiculous."

"It's a mark of respect, that's all."

"I don't see why Megan should respect me. She hardly even knows me."

The silver spoon drove into the fruit. "I don't see why she shouldn't," said my mother.

"Oh for goodness' sake." I poked at my grapefruit. "Where's Sharon, anyhow?"

"She'll be in in a minute. Megan, your elbow is on the table."

"Where's her place? Won't she be eating with us?"

"No."

"Isn't she here?"

"I imagine she eats with her family, after she goes home," said my mother mildly.

"Sharon eats in the kitchen," said Megan at the same moment, then looked at my mother guiltily. She hadn't meant to contradict her.

I pushed my chair back. The rosy bramble-patterned Wedgwood dishes rattled ominously. "Excuse me," I said. "If you don't mind, I'm going to ask her to join us." I rounded the table.

"Melanie, I'm sure Sharon is busy with dinner."

I paused and turned. Megan was pretending not to notice what was happening. "Then I'll just say hello to her."

"I'll ring if you want to see her."

"Ring?" With a blink of surprise I saw there was a bell by her place, a small silver bell with a long ivory handle.

"Yes."

"You don't really ring for her, do you? She's right on the other side of the kitchen door."

"Melanie—"

"Just a minute." The bell tinkled behind me as I pushed through the swinging door to the kitchen. "Sharon?"

Sharon Dennison stood before me, dressed in a black cotton uniform with a white apron, a heavy silver tray in her hand. "Was that the bell?"

I went in. "Sharon?"

"Hello. Did I hear the bell?" She gave me a freezing smile, as one might a professional colleague whose methods one deeply disapproved, then stepped carefully around me. In the dining room I heard her ask if they were finished with the first course.

"I suppose so."

A minute later Sharon again passed through the doorway, the three grapefruit dishes balanced on her tray. "Sharon."

She paused to glance at me. The door fell shut behind her. She was thin and dark, small-boned, with neatly fringed eyes the color of a room lit by television.

"Sharon, who told you to serve like a waitress?" Her chilly eyes flickered away from me.

"What? Excuse me, I have to get the chicken." I followed her through the large kitchen. She set the tray down, beginning to assemble the main course.

"Do you do this when Donald is around?"

65

"Do what?" She had a funny voice for a Dennison, kind of nasal and hard. "'Scuse me." She reached around me into a cabinet for a gravy boat and some bowls.

"Dress like that," I said, suppressing my annoyance at her extraordinary coldness. Slowly I understood it wasn't assumed on my account, or directed at me. She was just like that. "Wait on them," I added.

She shrugged. "Why not?" She put on an oven mitt, opened the oven and removed the chicken. A burst of tarragon filled the air. The oven door abruptly banged shut by itself.

"Donald puts up with this?"

"He does."

I leaned against a bank of pine cabinets. "I don't get it."

She didn't answer except to say Excuse me again. She took a ladle out from a drawer behind me. The kitchen was about ten degrees hotter than the rest of the house. The scent of tarragon was suffocating.

"Why do you go on with this?"

"It's my job."

"Yes, well a job is one thing, but this stuff about bells and eating in the kitchen—"

She paused. "What about it?"

"My mother doesn't want you to marry Donald, don't you see?" I lowered my voice. "She wants to humiliate you."

Sharon stared at me briefly, then laughed. She took a pot of carrots off the stove and began to dish them into a serving bowl. "You don't say," she muttered.

"What?"

"I said Tell me about it. Your mother, I mean." Sharon stood on her toes to peer into a cabinet. "She hates me."

"Oh, I don't think she hates you."

66

"She'd rather die than see Donald and me get married."
She shut the cabinet again without taking anything out.

"Well . . ."

"Oh come off it. She sent Donald to Europe to get him
away from me."

"I thought he was on sabbatical."

"Nupe." She poured the gravy into the boat. "Your
mother paid for him to go. She begged for him to go."

"Begged him?"

"Ayuh." She flashed me a humorless smile. "Out of sight
out of mind, don't you know. Could I get by you? I have
to take this stuff inside."

I picked up the now filled gravy boat and followed her
out the door. "Mother, did you send Donald to Europe?" I
sat down, this time unfolding my napkin.

"I beg your pardon?"

"Did you? To keep him from Sharon? She says—"

"Melanie, we can discuss this later." She glanced emphatically at Megan (who calmly, scrupulously ignored her),
then glared at me. I saw light.

"Don't tell me Megan doesn't know her father and
Sharon are getting married? You haven't been keeping this
a secret from her—?"

"Melanie." My mother's long spine was as straight as a
pinstripe. "You are making things very difficult."

Megan looked at me blankly, then looked at her grandmother. Secret or not, I was sure she had known this was
in the wind. She wouldn't even meet my eyes again though.
She knew which side her bread was buttered on. More important for a child, she knew who held the knife.

"Why did you do that?" I more or less screeched. "Why
do you make these secrets?"

"I think we can take this up later, all right?" My mother

glanced expressively at Sharon, then me. Sharon meanwhile was serving dinner politely, her small face completely impassive.

"But it's—All right. All right." I sank into silence, literally biting my tongue to maintain it. My mother launched into a Carson-like monologue, mostly chitchat about the neighbors and real estate and what kind of winter they'd had. She never did ask me about L.A., or Michael, or Helicon. I don't know why. She did get around to New York again though. After a while she asked about Jules.

"Has he helped you adjust to the city?" she inquired.

"Not much," I muttered, too peevish to be diplomatic.

"No?" She instantly set her fork and knife down as if to pay full attention to me. My answer seemed to concern her greatly. "He isn't supportive?"

"No, not especially," I said, with a lilting sarcasm meant to make light of her sudden concern. Then, ashamed of my hardness in the face of her anxious gaze, I explained, "In practical terms he's been helpful. He got the apartment and all that for me. It's just . . . in terms of emotional support he's been a little," I looked for a neutral word, "conservative."

"You mean he doesn't take care of you?" She leaned forward as if about to take hold of my hand. Her face, her voice, her attitude all telegraphed the tenderest solicitude. My report seemed deeply to disturb her. Seduced into telling the truth I burst out almost tearfully:

"No, not at all. That's just it, he's not even a bit sympathetic. I really think he doesn't want me to be in New York, to be honest."

"Oh." She leaned back. Her eyes went empty. "Well. That's how life is. There's no one to trust. You can't expect people to stand by you, really."

My mother. Iris used to call this maneuver of hers conversational judo. And quite rightly. I felt I'd revealed not only my own disappointment in Jules but also, disloyally, his unkindness to me. This was a private issue between us I hadn't even discussed with him yet. I certainly never intended to share it with my mother—though in fact she didn't seem to make much of it. My self-revelation, made in hopes of winning consolation, had gained me nothing but another slice of Mom's unbeatable home-baked despair. It was as if, offering me her hand to hold, she had taken mine and flipped me over her shoulder.

"Not even family?" I asked, but without much enthusiasm. I was too deflated to defend Love with much vigor just then.

"I don't know," she replied listlessly, unwilling to be so impolite, I think, as to hold to this point when specifically challenged by her own daughter.

I glanced at Megan, who was watching her grandmother with great attention. "Well, I'd stand by Jules," I said. "Or Megan. Or you."

My mother patted my hand. "I'm sure you would, dear," she said absently. She didn't look at me. She stared through the window at the horizon as if the sad history of man were written there in block letters. Bleak doesn't start to describe it.

I kicked Megan under the table.

"What?" she squealed.

"Just saying hello." I smiled at her. "Tomorrow let's go out canoeing, okay?"

She eyed me uneasily. "Okay," she said.

After dinner I fled by instinct to the piano, my refuge

from all unpleasantness since age thirteen. The piano at Milk Lake is a Sohmer spinet that resides in a slope-roofed unpapered room at the very top of the house. It used to stand in the living room downstairs but my mother moved it up to the third story some years ago, to give me privacy to work when I came visiting, she said. The eager delight with which my arrival had been anticipated had not, somehow, inspired anyone to get the piano tuned. This room went unused and unheated in the winter, and in summer the sun slanted in through the window (a strange trapezoidal aperture unequipped with curtains or shades) all day long. These conditions coupled with the dampness of the Maine thaws were ruining the instrument at a tremendous rate. You might as well have dumped it into the lake itself. I tried the keys. It was wildly off. With a snort (I can snort pretty well sometimes) I slammed the lid shut again and seated myself on the creaky bench.

My mother had a passion for secrets. Tell her a secret and she was as pleased as if you had given her jewels from the sacred East. She was a regular Mata Hari. Others in the family caught the madness. Information snaked among us with the stealthy grace of a midnight prowler. Not to tell Megan that Donald was planning to marry Sharon Dennison was exactly my mother's idea of clever. She didn't tell me my father was dying either.

At our last meeting Sharon had been a steamy little high school girl of fifteen, her fine dark hair in an optimistic Veronica Lake part, her toenails thickly lacquered with a shiny chipped coat of fire-engine red. Brown dusty feet thrust into sandals, shins scratched and bruised because she still scrambled around in the woods. Hips and breasts just beginning to happen under a clingy jumper. No shirt, just sun-baked shoulders and a curving collarbone. Sharp little chin. Dark-lashed, diamond-shaped, blue Dennison eyes. She'd grown older, but without quite growing up. She would always be a girl, first young, then old. She screamed sexuality, however, now as then. No wonder my mother feared her. No wonder, too, that even Donald had noticed her.

Sometimes I think the world is made up of Armours and Dennisons and nothing else. Though not all chilly the way Sharon is, all the Dennisons are slight like she is, and quick, and dexterous, and effortlessly sexual. They understand objects. A Dennison girl can whip up a dress in an hour. A Dennison boy can install a washer or wire a room in the same time. What makes Armours reach for the Yellow Pages is simply pie to Dennisons. They're as thoroughly comfortable in this world as if they owned the place. Which is an interesting point, I think, because they don't own the place. Such property as comes into their hands either slips away as if to its own happier destiny or, like Dennison's One-Stop, hobbles eternally down some thin line between subsistence and absolute failure. While Armours prosper Dennisons wait to inherit the earth. It's a legacy unlikely to reach them. Even if it did I imagine the property would pass out of the family inadvertently before they could profit by it. I have seen Dennisons gain and lose as much as five thousand dollars in a single day. Benjy Dennison, with whom it has many times been my considerable pleasure to sport, came to L.A. on a drug junket once and dropped three ounces of cocaine down the garbage disposal. He was just getting ready to cut it when an earthquake struck. I guess a Dennison is about the last person on earth my mother would have wanted to graft to her family tree.

The light in the slope-roofed room got pink. The sun was starting to set. I was trapped. I was done for. I'd been at the Farm all of two hours and already I'd shut myself up at the farthest dead end of the house from the others, like a laboratory rat that had taken a wrong turn somewhere back in the maze. I hadn't even been down to the lake yet. It's true that Armours can't live with each other. Also we can't live with anyone else.

I stood up and leaned against the window, looking out. There was a rosy stain across the water. The leaves on the birches hardly moved. Sunset is the worst time of day for birches, I think. They look so uncomfortable. That pink glow on their white bark is embarrassment, not pleasure. Birches need strong morning light, or a wind or a rainstorm. Something to move around in.

Megan came out of the house as I watched. She stopped to kick a couple of pebbles into the tiny stream that fed the lake, then followed it almost to its mouth and stepped calmly across it. From where I stood I could see the long straight part in her curly, pigtailed hair, dividing one side from the other as carefully as if their mingling might cause great harm. She walked slowly along the shoreline, her arms folded over her thin chest, her feet making crunchy, pebbly noises I could hear through the stillness even up there. She was looking at her feet, not the lake or the sunset. Soon she was far enough along the shore to be under the trees that flanked our beach. She was heading west, in the direction of a large flat granite rock I used to hide out on during my childhood summers here. It juts into the lake a little but is almost concealed from the house by shrubbery. It had been my refuge then, my only private retreat from misery and muddle before I learned about the piano. Megan's bent head moved in and out from under the trees, dark and light, dark and light. She was far enough away now to look small and unreal to me. I couldn't hear her steps anymore. She was almost at my rock. When she got there she climbed out on it familiarly. She sat, her legs folded up underneath her, nearly invisible even to me who had seen her go there. It was her rock. I put my hands flat against the cool window-pane, pressing as if I could reach her through it. This was my family. I was home.

SEVEN

❧

BENJY DENNISON STUFFED a yellow blanket up over the metal curtain rod and pulled it down on the other side. "There," he said with a flourish. "Privacy. Now the bunnies and squirrels can't see you."

I sat on the bed in his two-room cabin, my naked back against the unsanded, splintery wall, clothes lying in bright splashes and pools around me.

"Thank you," I said.

"You're welcome." He stood in front of the window a moment, silhouetted against the yellow glow the blanket had now become, looking at me with friendly eyes. "It's nice to see you again," he said.

"Nice to see you."

The cabin, half a mile into the woods from anywhere, was cool even in midafternoon. A small plane grated overhead; then only the chatter and whoosh and thump of birds as they landed and scuffled on Benjy's tar-papered roof. The smell of pine came from everywhere, through the walls and from the walls themselves. "You look good," Benjy said.

"Thanks."

"It's very nice to see you."

"So you say."

Benjy took two steps and a leap and landed on the bed with a soft whump that made the springs rock back and forth. He straddled me, gave me a friendly, exploratory lick between the legs, and pulled me down underneath him as calmly as if I'd been a length of ticker tape. Then he tucked into me with all the proficiency and goodwill of his generous Dennison soul. I opened my mouth against his shoulder. The tickly ends of his fine black hair swept against my neck like the uneven tip of a dry new watercolor brush. Benjy's skin was brown and smelled of soap and heat. He hovered over me, kissing me, one hand crushed between us and the mattress, the other tracing the lines of my shoulders and face. "Such beautiful eyes," he said.

"You too."

"You shouldn't wander around here by yourself."

"Oh yeah?"

"The woods are full of wolves."

"I can see that."

"You're lucky this time I happened to find you."

"Uh-huh." He moved farther inside me. I pressed my hands against the small of his back. We made circles against each other, both clockwise from our point of view.

"Uh-huh."

"You're not a wolf?"

"Me? A wolf has teeth, like this." He bit me. "I'm the woodcutter, don't you know."

I smiled. The circles went solemnly on, like an old-fashioned eggbeater ticking through the notches of its gearwheel one by one by one. A minute later I laughed out loud, suddenly.

"What?"

75

"Nothing, just happy to see you."

But he seemed suspicious and dug into me harder, forcing my legs up and around him. He fumbled for my wrists, found them and moved them up over my head, clamped them down with both his hands and raised himself over me. The circles were canceled. It seemed to be time to give me a taste of It. He looked into my face, serious and fierce. "Don't close your eyes," he whispered.

I didn't.

"Don't look away."

"Okay."

He smiled; or rather, he bared his teeth. His face closed off. He let into me with a vengeance. The male of the species. I'm not exactly voluptuous: this kind of thing can get to be painful. My mind wandered away from the room. There was nothing personal happening here. I thought about chord inversions, remembered a phone number I'd had five years before. I recalled Benjy in front of my house in L.A., closing the trunk of my car on a hot day. I'd had a set of Calico plates then, nice ones. I closed my eyes and examined with interest the explosions of light and blood in my lids.

"Don't close your eyes," Benjy said hoarsely.

"Okay." I watched him.

"Stay with me."

"Okay."

But he wasn't there. His spirit was balled up inside of him, or had flown away through the tarry roof. I was the only one left in bed, unless you want to count this temporary visitor, irritated and distracted like a guest with a car that won't start returning to use the phone. My muscles tightened around him involuntarily. The theatricality of his voice and his eyes annoyed me. He was breathing harder than he had to. I wished he'd finish. Why is it always a battle? Even with Benjy, kindest of men. He finally came and dropped to my chest.

We were both damp and chilly. For an instant Benjy rested on top of me; then he rolled off onto his side, one arm trailing across my shoulders. In my ear, through my hair, I felt the warm, exaggerated rush of breath pouring out of his open mouth. After a minute he stirred and kissed first the tip of my ear, then my cheek. He was back. I liked him again. Neither he nor I bothered about my coming. I can't come with a man inside me. I just keep getting more and less excited, like those trick birthday candles you can't blow out.

"Benjy?"

"Yes."

"This is nice."

He slipped his arms around me and held me against him. I pulled the sheet up and Benjy kicked it off himself. His chest grew dry again and warm. I rested my head there, lips just brushing the crook of his arm, and opened my eyes to look, over the slope of his upper arm, at the blanketed window again. It was so like a Dennison to improvise a curtain. The blanket was pretty, its lemony wool shutting out the whole world except that fuzzy yellow glow of light.

"How long are you home for?" he asked.

"A month. Till September. You?"

He shrugged; my head rolled against his shoulder. I glanced up. His long face had regained its natural expression, interested and good-humored. "Couple of weeks, maybe months," he said. "I got to recoup my losses."

"Oh Benjy, you got burned again?"

"Sure did."

"Jesus. Why don't you quit dealing? You're so terrible at it."

He was silent a moment. "What else am I going to do?"

"Oh." The birds on the rooftop thunked and fluttered. "I moved to New York, you know," I said.

"Did you? You like it?"

"Haven't been there long enough to know yet. We'll see. Sharon didn't tell me you were here."

"Told me you were."

"You should have called me. I was so surprised to see you in the woods like that."

"You can see me there any day. In fact, if you want to stick around for supper I got a hare I was going to cook up."

"A hare? You mean like a rabbit?"

"Yes ma'am. Got it this morning."

My insides shriveled. "No thanks. Benjy, are you that broke? Can't you eat with your family?"

"I'd rather not. Anyway, hare is good. In Europe they eat it all the time. You don't have to be broke to eat it."

"Oh. Yes. Well you know me, just the same old candy-assed American. I should go home for supper anyhow; I've only been here a couple of days."

"You know you kind of remind me of a rabbit?" Benjy asked.

"I do? Oh Benjy, don't go on please."

"No, you do. I don't know why. I don't mean little and cute—"

"Oh God no."

"I mean—"

"Never mind," I said.

"I mean scared."

"Uh-huh."

He pulled me closer to him and brought his mouth down on mine. He gathered me up in his brown arms as if I were something broken in pieces, forcing my lips apart with his tongue, pushing so my head fell back awkwardly, licking my teeth and the inside of my cheeks. "I'll look after you now," he said. I shrank back a little but he kissed my neck. That sadness that sometimes came to me came to me now. I felt him rising against my thigh like the key to my empty apartment. Well. After a minute I stopped resisting and gave myself over to sex.

EIGHT

I DISCOVERED my mother was ruling Milk Lake with her famous Iron Hand. On my way home from Benjy's that day I more or less tripped over a small child playing by the side of our stream. This was Amelia, Sharon's daughter. I'd never met her before and she declined to speak to me now but I found Sharon inside, changing Megan's bed, and she gave me the lowdown.

"Usually my folks look after her," she said, "but they had to go to Portland today." I took hold of the far side of a sheet and tucked it under the mattress. Sharon came around and undid it. "She'd be in the house but your mother won't let her."

"Holy Jesus," I said.

"I see you found Benjy."

"I did?"

"Your shirt's buttoned wrong."

I looked down. So it was. While I corrected the error Sharon held Megan's pillow between her teeth and wiggled it into a new case. "Where's Megan?"

"Living room, with your mother," said Sharon, speaking

around the pillow so that she sounded like a drunken gangster. "Saturday's her birthday you know."

"No I don't know." I paused with my shirt half open.

"Well it is." She spat out the pillow and dropped it onto the bed, whacking it there with the flat of her hand as if it had sassed her. "You better get her a present."

"Man, that burns me. Now my mother knew I wouldn't remember. Why didn't she tell me?"

"Maybe she forgot to tell you, by accident."

"One of the nice things about growing up in my family," I said—more like hissed—this was a text I'd enlarged on before, and it made me furious, "is that, however God may run his universe, in this house there are no accidents. There is no forgetting. There are no mistakes. Theologians should tour this house; you could turn it into a resort. 'Meaningless in the cosmos? Visit Milk Lake.'" I slammed my fist sideward against a wall, a bad oratorical habit, at least from the point of view of my hands. It startled Sharon. She stared at me. "My mother remembers bobby pins she bought in 1953. She can tell you—she *might* tell you—what grade I brought home in algebra in 1965. She's impossible. Nothing escapes her. The one thing you never have to worry about is that something here happened simply by accident. There's no such thing as accident here: this is a Freudian's paradise."

Having thus relieved myself I departed pianowards to get the rest of it off my chest. At moments like these I play Beethoven mainly, the one fly in the ointment being that it was my mother who made sure I learned all that classical stuff. It sounded pretty awful, of course, the piano being still untuned; but no one was listening anyway.

I spent the next day getting Megan a gift, a handmade

guitar like the one Iris gave me when I was twelve (and which I promptly lost). Megan had no friends. She spent all her time reading novels Jules and Iris and I had left at the Farm, or hanging around my mother and Donald. She was ripe for an instrument. I had to go clear up the coast to get the thing on such short notice; I was gone five hours. Nobody missed me. My mother couldn't have cared less. She didn't need me to look after Megan at all, as I now realized. She just wanted me up there to bolster the anti-Dennison forces. As for her health, she continued to insist she was perfectly well: so much for my private motive for spending the month in Maine.

Poor Megan. Birthdays in my family are not for the meek. If you want a fuss made over you you have to fight for it, and even then you get the idea life would have been easier without you. One year my whole family forgot my father's birthday, himself included. It was weeks before anybody remembered. Iris seemed embarrassed by presents, as if she thought they should have been given to somebody else. Jules and I were the only ones who really went in for it seriously. My mother doesn't celebrate her birthday—Iris told me because *her* mother turned on her shortly after birth, deliberately leaving her behind on a streetcar. Jules says this is not true. Apocrypha hang from our family tree like Spanish moss: you can't tell.

In addition to the guitar Megan got a cable from Donald, a cake from Sharon, some songbooks from me and a box of personalized Cartier stationery from my mother, to write what to whom I do not know. That was the extent of the haul. She wasn't even allowed to have Sharon eat with us. She liked the guitar though. The next day I dragged her with me to Benjy's and gave her her first lesson. We had a pretty good time, the three of us. Megan let Benjy tickle her. We all went raspberry-picking. Megan found a newt and christened it Jaws and then lost it again. Benjy made us both daisy garlands. On the way home she and I sang "100 Bottles of Beer" all the way down to fourteen.

That was on Sunday. The following night marked the start of the anniversary of my father's death. I didn't usually pay much attention to that date but this year for some reason—maybe because it was the first summer I was in Maine at the time—I got the idea to light a Yahrzeit candle for him. My father was Jewish, a fact my society-minded mother liked to forget. If you want to know the truth I think they were both Jewish: she just permanently forgot about herself.

All the time I was a kid at home my father came and went like a ghost. He would pop up at a cousin's wedding, or descend, wrathfully, when Jules or Iris or I had done something wrong; but most of the time he was gone, making money, more an idea than a person. Often he was actually out of town on business trips; but even when he was home we hardly saw him. He was treated as a cross between an emperor and an invalid. It was my mother, of course, who instituted this policy. When my father came home from work in the evenings they would sequester themselves in the living room for an hour, so he could relax, she said. The children were not allowed in. At dinner the rules of conversation were strictly fixed to preclude any possible upset. After dinner they went out as often as not. So I barely knew him. Summers at Milk Lake we saw him on weekends, and Mother said he was Tired. Of my father the word Tired connoted both heroic exhaustion and dangerous flammability. They spent his vacations abroad together. In early childhood I conceived of my father as mysterious and awful and all-powerful; in fact, I rather confused him with the God of Abraham. As I grew up I thought of him more and more as simply a stranger. He died in Maine the summer of my fourth year in California—suddenly, as I thought, though I gather my mother expected it. I guess a lot of people grow up feeling their fathers are strangers to them.

That afternoon I asked my mother if she had a Yahrzeit candle in the house.

"What for?" she asked.

"I want to light it for Daddy tonight."

"What for?"

"Because he died nine years ago tonight. I want to mark it."

"That's not necessary dear. There's an eternal flame burning for him at the temple in Sands Point. Didn't you know?"

"What is the significance of this so-called eternal flame?" I asked.

"It means we remember him perpetually," she said shortly.

"If it means we shouldn't light a candle for him," I said, "I can't help thinking it means we can forget him."

"What are you saying, Melanie?"

"I'm not saying anything." I'd found her in the dining room going through a small stack of bills and receipts. Now she put down her pen and pushed aside her checkbook. She folded her hands on the polished table in front of her and looked hard at me. "I just want to light a candle. Do you have one?"

"No I don't. We don't do that."

"What do you mean, we don't do that?"

"We don't light candles in this house."

"Well I light candles in this house. I'm going to light one tonight, for example. For my father."

"Melanie, that's preposterous. It's not even the proper date."

"Yes it is," I said. "August fourth, right?"

"On a Christian calendar, yes. But if you're observing a Jewish ritual you should observe it when it falls in the Jewish year. It isn't the same."

"Interesting," I said, "but not significant. Since you don't have a candle would you lend me the car please so I can go get one?"

"No. I can't."

"Excuse me?"

"I'm sorry, but I need the car now. I'm going out."

"You're doing your bills."

She got up and left them. "Keep an eye on Megan, will you? And tell Sharon I'll be back for dinner."

She left.

I went with Megan to Dennison's One-Stop, on foot, and bought—not a Yahrzeit candle, of course, they wouldn't have had such a thing—but the tallest fattest candle there. Amelia Dennison was playing at her grandfather's feet by the cash register. She'd talk to Megan (what few words she knew) but still not to me. I don't know why she held so aloof from me; mostly Dennisons like me. I blushed when Mr. Dennison handed me my change. Besides fooling around every chance I got with Benjy, I lost my virginity to his older son, Prescott Junior, thirteen years ago. I still don't know if he has any idea.

That evening I lit the candle in secret, setting it in a saucer on the varnished window seat in my room. Night fell quickly. I repeated the one line of the mourner's kaddish I could remember five or six times and sat for a while watching the flame. It did seem like a human life: it had light and heat and only so many hours to burn. I put my hand over the rise of air above the flame and it felt like touching my father. Of course my ignorance of the ritual was pathetic—I felt about on a level with a movie savage worshiping an airplane or cherishing a bit of colored glass—but this was the best I could do. I was too scared of fire to let it burn all night unwatched and finally had to blow it out before I slept. I felt as if I were snuffing my father. I figured he and God and I would just have to try to understand each other as best we could. In the morning I lit the candle again. The piano tuner came and I played a little. I lay low the rest of the day.

A letter from Lucian arrived Wednesday—postage due of course—in an envelope torn open and resealed with Scotch tape. My mother brought it in to me, scanning it with her camera-eyes. "Isn't that your new address?" she asked. "Who's Lucian Curry?"

"Nothing, it's a joke," I said, taking it and departing for my room. I read the letter on my bed. Lucian wrote in a fat, unpracticed, sloping cursive that rushed forward as if the consonants were trying to leap over the vowels. Half the sheet was covered with news about New York and acting classes and how was I and how was he, Love, Lucian. Then: "P.S. I wrote this at Ivory's but I'm finishing it here at your place. God I'm glad you left your key. I won't go into details. Can you come home early maybe? I need to see you so bad." This was in pen. Then in pencil beneath it: "Damn, I can't find anything except a thirteen cent stamp. I guess this got there anyway. I love you. L."

86

The only private phone in the house was in my mother's bedroom—and so was my mother. Sharon had gone grocery shopping and Megan was out by the lake playing her guitar so I figured the phone in the kitchen would do me. I sat for a minute longer and reread the letter, then went downstairs. My line was busy at first. I waited a minute, drumming on the oaken table with my index fingers, thinking with dread of the ping-pong volley of questions and answers that would surely follow my explaining to Mother who Lucian was. The plot had thickened. I was intrigued. I tried him again and he picked up.

"Lucian, it's me."

"Hello? Melanie?"

"Yes, is something wrong? You sound strange."

"No, it's just—I thought it might be your mother again. She just called me you know."

"Excuse me?"

"She just called here, your mother. Trying to dial your brother, she said, and dialed you by accident. I wonder who she thought I was."

Outside Megan switched endlessly back and forth from A^7 to E^7.

"Oh for Christ's sake."

"What did you say?"

"I can't talk to you now. Just tell me if you're okay."

"You called me to say you can't talk now?"

"I called to see if you needed anything, but Lucian, for all I know my mother's on the extension upstairs right now."

"But she said she was calling your brother."

"We're on the only line up here."

"Oh," he said. "Well I'm fine. Ivory and I are finished. I

had the worst week of my life, just about, but I'm fine now. Can't you come back for a day even?"

"Maybe."

"That would be so wonderful."

"You have my number here anyway." I hesitated a minute, divided between my desire to take care of Lucian and my desire to tear my mother's throat out. "Look Lucian," I finally said, "I don't think you should split up with Ivory unless you're completely ready, you understand? There's something a little brave in your voice I don't like."

"At times you have to be brave."

"Yeah, well, I notice if you're too brave you tend to end up worse off than before. Trust me, I've been through this one. Don't be a hero, okay?"

"I'm not speaking to him," he said sullenly. "It's over."

"Okay."

"You know? In fact, let's don't even talk about Ivory."

"Okay."

"I just want to get on with my life, you know?"

"Okay. I'll be in touch."

"Having your key pretty near saved me. I mean it."

"Then I'm glad I left it."

"I love you."

"Why do you say that?" I asked, despite my concern that my mother was listening. Let her listen.

"I do."

"Well Lucian . . ." I fumbled for words. Then a thought struck me suddenly. "Do you have any money?"

"Some."

"I left two hundred dollars in the piano bench. Open it up. See it?"

"Yes, just a—yes, here it is."

"I'll send more tomorrow."

"I don't—"

"I left it for you, Lucian. If you don't need it, don't use it."

"I'll pay it back."

"I know. I better go."

I stormed my mother's rose-covered fortress. "That was low."

"Low?"

"Calling my place."

"What do you mean, dear?"

"Jesus." She sat in her squarish armchair, feet on the ottoman, thin and frail, a copy of *The Women's Room* open in her narrow lap. Her phone was on the nightstand, the receiver innocently resting in its cradle, all the way across the room. "I just spoke to Lucian."

"Who *is* Lucian?"

"He said you'd called him."

"Well, yes, I guess I must have. I was trying to reach Jules."

"Were you? Then why didn't you?"

"He wasn't home, dear," she said, eyes mild and wondering.

"For Christ's sake—"

"I'm sorry I called your apartment Melanie. I really don't see why it's so terrible. It was an error, that's all. Your new number is right under Jules's in my book, after all, and the exchange is the same."

"Never mind," I broke in. "I'm going up—"

The phone rang.

"I'll get it." I charged across to the nightstand, thinking it might be Lucian again. At least if my mother was in sight she could only hear half the conversation. But it wasn't Lucian; it was Donald. I said hello and started to give the phone to my mother.

"No, wait," he said, his voice distinct and tiny through the overseas connection. "Melanie? I hoped you would pick up. Listen, I'm coming home."

NINE

☙❧

As soon as I'd hung up the phone my mother asked, "Why is he coming back?" For some reason her face turned a smudgy gray, like the color a dirty eraser leaves on a sheet of white paper.

"He's unhappy."

"You should have let me talk to him."

"He didn't want to."

"I knew that was him the minute the phone rang," she said dreamily, as if this made her a prophetess.

"Then you were right." I left her alone.

If you listen to Donald this was a critical moment in my mother's life. Of course if you listen to Donald all kinds of things are critical: human actions are like huge stone dominoes falling against one another in endless slow motion, crashing and making the earth shake as if the world were no sturdier than a jerry-built bungalow. Not a great thinker, Donald, mind you; but there's something seductive about his vision that makes it advisable not to listen to him too long.

Of course he'd come back to marry Sharon—that was the point. I picked him up at the airport. He looked like hell, his green eyes raw-rimmed and shot with blood as if he'd been swimming, cheeks the translucent blue of an aerogramme, blond hair thin and not clean. He hadn't slept on the airplane, he said, and he hadn't shaved since England. Donald's beard grows in funny, in two discrete stripes on each cheek, like sky-blue warpaint. He's a small man, hardly taller than I am, given to wearing work shirts and frayed corduroys. His clothes hung loosely on him now. He and my mother had worn each other down to the bone, I think.

He made his announcement just before dinner, Sharon by his side. As far as I was concerned the snail was back on the thorn, Young Love restored to its throne, God in his Heaven, etc., etc. Even my mother seemed to take the turn of events with becoming philosophy. From the far reaches of the cellar, with her own leaflike hands, she retrieved a bottle of excellent port to toast the happy couple. This was the first time Megan had been allowed to drink; everyone teased her. Sharon sat at the dinner table finally, and very pretty she looked too, in the glow of Donald's tired eyes. The wedding was set for September. I was elected a bridesmaid, a nice goodwill gesture I thought considering Sharon was not entirely crazy about me.

After dinner I felt sort of crummy and crawled out into the woods to see Benjy. This is possibly graceless but I can only take so much prenuptial merriment before I get a stomachache. Anyhow I'd only seen Benjy once since Sunday, and that had been all too brief; I set off to find his cabin by flashlight. The trail was unmarked, so my journey there was no treat—of course he didn't have a phone or anything like one—and when I got there I found the place dark. This was not my night. Benjy had left a note for me punched over the handle of the door (it didn't exactly have a knob) dated Wednesday, saying he'd gone to Houston. A drug run, no doubt. I leaned my head against the pine boards. He said he'd be back in two or three days.

The night was warm and clear, the woods full of those interesting snaps and rustles you never hear in the daytime. A mosquito had the nerve to land on my cheek; I destroyed it. I sat down to think for a minute on the boxlike step to the cabin. A nearby owl asked its usual question. The usual Armour question is Why. I planted my moccasined feet in front of me and buried my hands in the pouch of my sweatshirt. They met each other inside with surprise. There was no point in my staying in Maine now: my scene in this drama was finished. I figured I'd hang around through the weekend and see Benjy again, then leave on Monday. I went home to call Lucian and tell him.

It seemed remarkable to be able to do that—that it wasn't too late to call him, I mean. In Maine it was the middle of the night. Everyone was in bed. In New York Lucian was just on his way out for the evening. I felt as if I were phoning a different planet.

"Where are you going?"

"Just out to a bar. What's up?"

I told him I was coming down Monday. "I'll need you to be there, okay? You have my key."

"Sure, okay. Boy, I'm glad you're coming."

"I figure I'll land in New York about four. Any time after four, is that all right?"

"For sure. I could come out to the airport and meet you—"

"No no, it's easier this way. Just be there. You're sure you can be there?" I was waiting for him to say he had to be somewhere with Ivory but he didn't. Apparently Ivory was still benched.

Mother came up to chat with me next morning. "I guess

you'll be wanting to go home now," she said.

"I beg your pardon?"

"You'll want to go home. Don't feel you have to stay."

"Have to?"

"Well, it does make a lot of work for Sharon, and now that she's getting married she'll need time—"

"One second. Back up," I said, sitting up in bed. I hadn't even gotten up yet. "Did you just say I'm making work for Sharon?"

"An extra person in the house, Melanie—"

"You must be joking."

"Certainly I'm not joking. When Donald was gone there was a reason for it. But now—"

"Wait a minute, this interests me. What kind of work exactly do I require?"

"Extra bed, extra mouth . . ." she said, waving a vague hand. "Of course, when Megan needed looking—"

"Extra what? You know sometimes I think you are stark raving nuts."

"Why are you getting so upset?" she asked reasonably, sitting down on the bed. "I'm just suggesting that since you must be eager to settle into your new apartment—"

"You're throwing me out, aren't you?"

"Don't be silly." She made a gesture as if to smooth down an obstreperous air current. "I simply—"

"You haven't given up at all. You want me out of the way so you can work Donald over in peace. You've stepped off the curb Mother, you really have."

"Melanie, if you could express yourself calmly I'd be very much obliged."

I sat bolt upright. "You're actually throwing me out."

"I'm not throwing you out, for heaven's sake. You're wel-

94

come to stay as long as you like. This is your home—"

"This is not my home," I said hotly.

She stood up. Apparently I had offended her deeply. "I don't care to continue this discussion," she said quietly, and left the room without closing the door.

"I'm out of here in two hours," I shouted after her, throwing off the covers. I jumped out of bed and ran to the door. "Two hours," I repeated defiantly, apparently under the misapprehension that this signaled a dreadful defeat for her. I was in Connecticut before I realized the reverse was true.

One of the things I learned in L.A. was how to do things fast. Within ninety minutes I was up, dressed, packed, had decided to drive down—another souvenir of L.A., this desire to drive when impassioned—had reserved a rental car, told Sharon and Donald I was going, dragged Megan out with me to Benjy's cabin to leave a note for him, and tried to let Lucian know I was coming early. I couldn't get through to him though—no answer. I figured I'd catch him from the road.

Donald was to drive me to Avis. My mother had vanished into her bedroom. I knocked and she serenely invited me in. She was sitting upright in her rose-ridden armchair, a pink and white afghan across her lap. On her knees was an Eaton Connoisseur writing kit; I could see the salutation. She was starting a letter to Norman Flexner. "I'm going," I said.

"Are you sure you won't stay for lunch?"

"No thank you."

"Well then. Drive safely." She looked up, distracted, then set the kit aside on the table, next to the cut-crystal vase of fresh roses, and held up her arms for me to kiss her.

95

I touched my lips to the powdery cheek. It was cool and disconcertingly yielding. That was age. The heat and flesh of life were failing her. In spite of my fury a thin, clear stream of sadness and tenderness for her suddenly flowed through me. The mortal envelope I'd just kissed couldn't seal her away from death forever, not even for forty more years, probably not twenty—maybe not ten. Whatever she was, she was just as much at the mercy of time as anyone. I put my lips to her cheek to kiss her good-bye again very gently. Unfortunately the unexpected movement startled her and she lifted her hand in confusion, reflexively, meaning to brush away whatever it was that was coming at her. As I straightened she tried to cover the gesture by patting her hair with both hands. No one was fooled. I left the room on a wave of anger and heard her call out good-bye again only over its growing roar.

TEN

≫≪

WHEN I ARRIVED at my apartment in New York there was nobody inside it. The lights were off, the door locked. I'd tried again and again to get Lucian on the phone, all the way down the coast, but there'd been no answer. I'd dawdled interminably through Massachusetts, but to no avail. Reluctantly, I left my suitcases in the vestibule of my building and walked over to Jules's. It took him a while to answer his door, which gave me time to decide on my story. To minimize confusion I told him I'd left my key in Maine by accident.

"Smart move."

"It was nothing." Modesty, that's the note you want to strike.

He rubbed at his face with a terry-cloth sleeve. My brother has the most terrible looking robes I've ever seen. "What time is it?"

"I don't know. Two. Three. Give me the key and go back to bed."

He went to a drawer in his desk and rummaged around a while. "Why are you down here anyhow?"

"Donald came back."

"Oh yeah, I heard." He found my key and handed it to me. His feet were bare on the nubbly mud-colored carpet. Languorously he scratched one foot with the toes of the other. "Norman called me."

"Flexner? How'd he know?"

"Mom called him. This morning. Yesterday. Whatever. She was all bent out of shape, he said."

"That sounds like her."

"She called him . . . he called me . . ." Jules yawned. "Why are you here now? Are you okay? You could stay here—"

"No thanks. I better get home. Sorry about this." I started to leave.

"Maine all right?"

"Peachy. Go to bed, I'll call you tomorrow. Today."

Jules yawned again and waved at me sleepily. I walked back to my place not thinking, dead tired. When I got there I was astonished to find the door open, the lights on, my Chopin tape running inside, and Lucian standing in the doorway. My heart leaped up.

"I saw your suitcases but they didn't register at first," he said, throwing his arms around me. He kissed me. "Then I realized. God, when'd you get here? Why didn't you call me?"

"I called you all day. I got here just now."

"But how come? I thought you weren't—"

"My mother and I had a fight." I still remember what Lucian looked like to me that night, so solid, so beautiful. "Let's go inside," I said.

He said Um.

"Why, what's in the apartment? Oh tell me you haven't destroyed it, please," I said, walking in past him.

"No, it's just that—"

"Hello?" In my living room on the piano bench sat a man, about forty or so, looking politely but curiously back at me. He was elegant, spare, with a half-smile of amusement hovering behind his dry, set mouth. "Ivory?" I asked without meaning to.

Lucian said quickly, "Melanie, this is Rupert."

"Rupert?" I thought, from his age I suppose, it must be some friend of Ivory's.

The man stood up and extended a neat, square hand. He was clearly wondering what I was doing there. "Rupert Brophy," he said.

"Oh really?" We shook hands.

"Rupert, Melanie Armour. Rupert's a painter, Melanie."

"Yes, I know."

"Do you know each other?"

"No, I know his—I know your work. Everybody knows his work. Lucian, why is Rupert Brophy in my living room?"

Immediately he started to blush, then to blush more because he was blushing. "It's—"

"Is this your living room?" Rupert asked, eyebrows high.

"Yes, rather."

"Lucian told me—"

"I didn't realize—"

"Of course we've only just met, you see," said Brophy, still standing. He looked mildly at Lucian. "Ought I to leave?"

The truth gradually dawned on me. I'd been so concerned to comfort what I'd thought was Lucian's aching heart that it hadn't occurred to me. "Oh gracious me, not on my account," I said, looking daggers at Lucian.

"Yes, I think I had best," Rupert Brophy went on, crossing to the door. "Charming to meet you. Lucian?" He said the name Lucian with three syllables.

Lucian glanced at him helplessly. "I didn't expect—"

"Yes, I see that," said Brophy. Delicately he nodded to me. His smile was all urbanity. "You don't mind, I hope?" He went to Lucian and kissed him deliberately on the mouth. "You have a nice touch," he said, looking at me, then the piano, then the tape recorder, then Lucian. He left, closing the door gently.

"Hi," I said to Lucian. He sank to the empty floor and sat, hugging a Calvin-Kleined knee to his chest.

"Hi," he said.

I snapped off the recorder. "Not cramping your style, I hope?"

"What?"

"I could leave," I went on.

"What's the matter?" he asked. "Sit down. I'm so glad to see you."

"I doubt that."

His soft blue pinstriped shirt was half open. His linen jacket was flung across the piano, and his heavy boots had collapsed to their sides by the pedals. A box of matches and a half-smoked joint leaned against each other in the lid of a jam jar. Nearby, a tightly rolled twenty-dollar bill unfurled by slow degrees. An unopened bottle of Grand Marnier sat at the top of the stairs. The paper bag in which it had been brought from the store lay screwed up on top of the little brick table, beside it the two liqueur glasses I'd bought for our first supper three weeks before. Over the music rack of the piano hung a peach-colored raw silk tie. We both saw it at once. "Oh shit," said Lucian. "That's Rupert's."

"No kidding. Excuse me, I need some water." I went into the kitchen, splashed my face, drank, bathed my eyes. When I came back Lucian had moved his jacket and boots and the tie into a corner. I sat down several yards from him. "This is really terrific," I said.

"What's the matter?" he asked again. "Is there something the matter?"

"The matter is, I've been driving all night and I come home to find I can't get into my place—"

"If you'd called—" said Lucian.

"I did call, I called all day. Where were you?"

"Out."

"Out, what is out? All day?"

"Yes, all day. Listen Melanie, do you want an explanation or something? I mean it's too bad I wasn't here—"

"I'll say. I just woke up my brother to get my key. Now what am I supposed to do when I get back here and find—"

"Find what? What did you find?"

"One of the prominent artists of our day with his hands in the jeans of my favorite waif?"

"He didn't have his hands in my—" He didn't finish the sentence, he just smiled and looked down at the floor.

We were silent a while. The twenty-dollar bill unrolled noiselessly. "I thought you were getting over Ivory," I said.

"I am."

"I was worried about you."

"Well, thank you. This is how I get over a breakup, okay?"

"What, picking up strangers?"

"It works."

"It's—unattractive," I said.

"What do you mean, unattractive? Sordid?"

"You could say sordid." I actually accused him of this, I, who have wandered home any number of times with men I wouldn't eat lunch with the following day.

Lucian made an effort to restore perspective. "Look," he said, uncrossing his legs, "let's don't argue about this now, okay? We're both tired. Sex is sex. It is what it is. It has nothing to do with us; or with anything else for that matter."

I laughed at him, stood up and went to the vestibule. "To me," I said, bringing in both my suitcases, "sex is not just sex, it does have something to do with the rest of life, and you don't go around fucking strangers."

"You do if you're gay," he said.

"I'm not gay." I left one valise by the door and started to carry the other downstairs. At the top of the steps was the Grand Marnier bottle. "How did you get this far in ten minutes?" I muttered. I wanted to kick the bottle down before me but I only shoved it aside with my foot. It ricocheted against the doorjamb and almost toppled over, then settled on its base with an uneven flurry of rotating thuds. "Half an hour ago you weren't even here."

"What?" He had gotten my other suitcase and was starting to follow me down.

"Don't."

"Excuse me?"

"Don't bother with my things. I'll take care of them."

"Melanie? What's wrong? Talk to me."

I went down the stairs alone and set the valise by the door to the bedroom. The bed was unmade. I started back up. Lucian stood waiting for me midway up the staircase. "What's wrong is I'm in a thumping bad mood, I realize I should never have asked you to stay here, I'm sorry, and I want you to leave. Okay?"

"Leave for where?"

"For wherever," I said.

"Are you serious?"

"Dead." I decided to get the other suitcase in the morning. I wanted to sleep. The chute I had slipped down my first night here opened again before me. I went down to my bedroom without looking back at Lucian, took off my jeans and rolled into bed. The sheets smelled of skin and hair, his. Gray daylight filtered through the air, threatening more light minute by minute. I buried my face in the pillow.

"Melanie?" Lucian said. I felt his warm hand softly laid on my shoulder. "Melanie, could you talk to me please?"

"I'm asleep. You go back to Ivory."

"I can't go back."

"Fine. I'm sleeping, okay?"

"I saw Ivory yesterday, in a café, just by chance. He told me he despises me. That's what he said."

"Okay with me," I said into the pillow.

"He told me I'm ungrateful. I think he thinks he bought me."

"Well?"

Lucian took his hand from my shoulder. He said slowly: "You can't buy me."

I considered this for a moment. I turned over.

"Melanie, please be my friend. I need a friend." He sat down on the bed beside me and touched my hair, then suddenly bent and pressed against me, lifted me up in his arms, kissed my cheek. "I didn't mean for this to happen." He laid me down again, still bending close over me. "Don't think badly of me, will you? I know you think I'm a—a heathenist or something—"

"Hedonist." I shut my eyes.

"Hedonist. But I'm not. When you're gay, it's just different. That's how it is."

"Uh-huh."

"It is. Ivory was with someone else too."

"Uh-huh."

"It really hurt me."

I turned my face away toward the other pillow. "Maybe you shouldn't break off with him yet."

"No, it's over. I'm just really glad to see you."

I opened my eyes to find myself staring into the shadow under the second pillow. I lay unmoving a moment. Lucian's hands, warm and insistent, still held my shoulders. He leaned down and kissed my cheek again. Instinctively I turned my face up to him. "Okay," I said, feeling as if I were surrendering to the sadness yet somehow escaping it at the same time.

He sighed his relief. "God, I love you." He jumped up from the bed. "I just got such a great idea."

"What?"

"I can't tell you. I'm going out for a little while."

"Really? It's four in the morning."

"Well I'm a little bit, um, coked up . . . I don't think I could sleep right now."

"I see."

"And anyway, I've got this wonderful idea. I'll be right back—I mean, you go to sleep, and when you wake up you'll see."

"What is it?"

"Just go to sleep now," he said, more or less dancing out

the door. "You'll see later."

ᴥ

When I woke up my bed was covered with flowers. The floor, every square inch of it, was covered with flowers, leaves, sprays, stems. Lucian was standing in front of the glass doors, very pleased with himself, up to his ankles in daisies. He'd stared me awake. He just couldn't wait any longer to show me what a clever boy he'd been and to see me look amazed. He got what he wanted. "I went to the flower market," he said. "What do you think?"

"Oh Lucian."

"I'm going to make breakfast too, breakfast in bed, whatever you want. Okay?"

Spread over me was a tangled quilt of roses, chrysanthemums, sweet william, daisies . . . "Oh Lucian. Jesus. I don't—" I broke off to lean down and snuffle my way through the leafy blanket.

"I bought an iris too. For Iris. Just one. Is it okay?" He pointed to a glass in the corner in which the single flower stood.

"Jesus Christ. Just when I thought you were hopeless."

"I'm not hopeless; God. Tell me what you want for breakfast. I bought bread and eggs and milk and bacon so tell me whatever you want, okay? You want eggs?"

"Sure, fine. Could you come here and kiss me?"

He did so impatiently. His eyes were pink from sleeplessness. "Come on, I'm starving. Tell me what you want. How do you like your eggs?"

"Fried?"

"Okay. And bacon and toast? I bought blackberry jam, you think it'll be good?"

"Sure, yes, whatever you like. Look, I'll get up and help. You don't have to cook breakfast all by yourself."

"No, that's the whole idea is you stay here and just smell things while I cook. Want orange juice?"

"You bought orange juice?"

"I bought everything," he said, bounding out of the room. A minute later he bounded back in, or rather, his bright face appeared at the doorway, obscured by a stratus cloud of sheepishness. "Melanie?"

"Yes my dear."

"How do you make fried eggs?"

"You fry them."

"Fry?" As though I'd said amortize, or manumit.

"I'd better help you."

"No."

I slipped carefully out of my bed and shuffled through the flowery carpet. "Fried eggs. From the Latin fry, or fry, and the English egg. Meaning, to eat an egg. Generally speaking you don't bake bacon, however."

"I know that. I just didn't know—what about your flowers?"

"We'll come back and eat down here." I followed him up the steps. "I don't want you putting toes in the toast."

"Melanie, please—"

"Or Jews in the orange juice. 'Please' yourself. I don't suppose you bought butter by any chance?"

He echoed blankly, "Butter?"

I rolled up the sleeves of the shirt I'd been wearing since I put it on at Milk Lake. "Stand aside."

I went into the kitchen.

ELEVEN

SIX WEEKS OF happiness followed.

I want to say a little about what it meant to me to live in New York City. New York was grown up. It demanded self-sufficiency; it conferred legitimacy. You walked alone among millions. Each day you passed a thousand lives and never turned your head. You had to have focus. You had to have purpose. Otherwise you drowned. To live in New York was the ultimate in independence, the last word in authenticity. It dared you to build an identity while every day dangling you over an abyss of anonymity. Like the army. On the flip side of the same single was the fact of being in reality wholly isolated, though in appearance surrounded by people. If you could make it work for you, you were a person, a real person, valid. If you went under, that was failure.

Though I had grown up close to the city, this idea of New York had always terrified me. I'd never felt substantial enough to hold my own within it: even my little business trips there during the time I lived in L.A. had been more or less harrowing. People actually live in L.A. They're born and they die there, raise their families there. I know this is true of New York too, but it seems impossible. The *New York Times* doesn't even print a comics page. You can make mistakes in L.A. New York is autocratic, imperial, absolute.

But here I was with this affectionate semichild in my house. What did that mean? Certainly it must be cheating. There was nothing in the rules about being entitled to the company of an interesting young man. I had come to New York prepared to claw my way through it tooth and nail. Now, at the first skirmish, New York had stuffed a flower in my mouth. What could I do? I savored the flower.

Of course, Lucian had done nothing about his monologue in my absence. He had been going to acting classes it seemed, and continued now; but the monologue had been forgotten. Once I was back his enthusiasm about it resurfaced. For a while, working on it was our principal pastime. Usually I would lie on the floor in the living room staring at the ceiling while Lucian paced circles around me. He enjoyed very much the appearance this gave him of being deep in thought. "We shouldn't have the guy in love with both the man and the woman, I think," he'd say. "You know, the actor guy. I mean, that's too—like, hockneyed—"

"Hackneyed. Hockney's the artist."

"Right. It's trite and sort of, um, pat. He should be under like an obligation to the man almost, you know? At least, the man thinks so—"

"The producer, you mean."

"Right, the older man. But the woman . . ."

He stopped, looking at me without seeing me. I was stretched out with my hands above my head, perfectly flat. It was mid-August now and the afternoon heat was simply unfair. We'd sealed up the house against it as if it were an evil demon. All our faith was in the air conditioner, whose steadfast singlenoted chant kept the beast at bay. The living room—still without furniture—was full of purple shadow. Lucian knelt down for a moment and put his hand on my arm. "You think it would be too weird to have the woman be like a hooker?"

I laughed. "What do you mean, like a hooker?"

"Not a streetwalker kind of hooker, a high-class mistress, I mean," he said, jumping up again and resuming his artistic-looking laps around the room. "She'd be mainly just a really nice girl, I mean—she could be young, maybe even the same age as he is—" He stopped moving suddenly. "Why don't you say anything? You think this is dumb?"

"Not if you want it that way."

"What do you mean by that way? You think I should have her be older than him?"

"Whatever you want."

"Well *help* me Melanie, don't just—don't just *lie* there."

"What do you want? How do you want it?" I sat up too abruptly and ended up feeling a little dizzy. "Do you want the woman to have seen more of life than the actor has? I thought you said he felt a kinship to her."

"Yeah—"

"So what kind of kinship would he feel to a hooker?"

"I don't know, he might feel something. Maybe they're both kind of—reckless, you know. Like, free people, outside the bounds of society."

"Terrific."

"What's the matter with that? A hooker is a kind of outlaw you know—like outside legitimate society."

"Right."

"Don't *agree* with me if you don't *agree* with me," he said, waving both hands excitedly. "If you don't think—"

"Well what about the actor? What kind of outlaw is an actor?"

"He's an artist, he's an outlaw by—"

"Oh for God's sake—Lucian, we're not going to discuss the artist as rebel, are we? What's the point of all this? I don't get why it matters if you're doing a five-minute monologue. How much of this story can possibly come out in a five-minute monologue?"

"You don't understand, I have to know everything, the whole thing, even if it doesn't come out. As an actor I need that, so even if the audience doesn't hear it in words they can *feel* it in my performance, don't you see?"

I sighed and lay down again. "Okay. So they're both reckless outlaws and she's really a nice girl."

"You're making fun of me."

"Bingo."

"You know what I think? Where's your tape recorder?"

"Downstairs."

Lucian shot down the staircase and vaulted back up again, the little cassette recorder under his arm. He plugged it in and put it on the floor near my shoulder. "There. Talk."

"What?"

"You're her. The girl. Talk."

"Oh man—"

"It's improvisation. You're the woman—Danielle. Okay? You're Danielle. I'm . . . Mick. No, Guy."

I laughed.

"You think Guy's too theatrical? How about, um . . ."

"What's the difference? It's a monologue. You're not going to apostrophize yourself, are you?"

"I have to *know*," he repeated, exasperated. "Melanie?"

"Yes."

"What about Kelly?"

"Is this being recorded?"

"Yes, why?"

"I wouldn't want to lose a word of it, that's all. On what cassette, by the way?"

"It's a blank cassette," he said impatiently, "don't worry." But he took it out, looked at it, and flipped it over. "Can't you help me think of a name at least?"

"All right. Kelly."

"No, you don't like that."

"Francis. Hey, is your real name Lucian Curry by the way? I've always wondered that."

He ignored the suggestion and the question. "Christopher. Chris. I like that. Yeah, that's good."

"Okay. Christopher."

"And you're Danielle."

"Right. Danielle."

"Okay. Let's talk. Don't talk as Melanie anymore."

"But what do you mean, let's talk?"

"I said don't talk as Melanie anymore!"

"But Lucian, where are we?"

"I'm not Lucian—"

"Where are we, how did we meet? What's going on? Why would I talk to you—"

"That's it!" he suddenly broke in, delighted. "That's exactly what we should decide. I think we meet . . . it should be somewhere unusual I think, you know, exotic. Maybe a beach in Brazil or . . ."

And so on. It took almost three weeks to finish it. Eventually the locale shifted to somewhere perfectly domestic, an apartment in the city; Danielle became Emily; Christopher went straight and was simply talking to his old girl-

friend—in short, the ordinary prevailed over the improbable.
The monologue stopped being about making a choice and
started being about getting used to one. In the final stages
Lucian actually worked on it alone, while I attended to my
own work. Patty Bates had suggested, with some embarrassment, that I come up with a song about a random killing,
preferably with a reggae beat. Random killings were very
big that season, especially with a reggae beat. I couldn't
really get behind it; in fact, all I seemed to be coming up
with were love songs. Everywhere I turned I came across
hooks for love songs, really nice ones, and two of the pret-
tiest melodies I ever came up with floated into my head in
those weeks. Living with Lucian agreed with me. He was so
beautiful. I looked at him and I felt good. Every morning
one of us went out for cinnamon rolls, then brought them
home to eat on the patio. In the evenings we went to movies
and plays, or sometimes we just stayed in. At the end of
each night we would sit and talk and yawn at each other
for half an hour or so; then, reluctantly, one of us would
announce he was off to bed. We never slept in the same
bed again. Lucian always kissed me good-night on the
mouth.

I couldn't write Jamaica Jugular, or whatever it was they
wanted. I ended up with four or five love songs instead.
Two of them, ballads—"Every Kind of Happiness" and "If
It's Only Me"—were about Lucian. Maybe they were all
about Lucian.

I taped the songs and sent them over to Patty. She called
and we made an appointment for me to come in the following week. She didn't say anything on the phone about the
tape, if she'd listened to it. My contract was due to expire
in a month.

Lucian at last performed his monologue for me the day before that meeting. I'd gone out to have lunch with Jules (Jules and Lucian had finally met the week before; it was not a pleasant occasion, and afterward I had to listen to much name-calling and innuendo on both sides—bloodless critic, faggot actor, that sort of thing) and had come back at three or so to find Lucian seated on the piano bench in the middle of the living room, an unplugged phone on the bench beside him. I'd interrupted him mid-scene; for a minute he was very disoriented. Then he decided to do the scene for me, got very excited, insisted on making me iced tea (which he accomplished by pouring hot water over an ice cube and a tea bag in a small cup) and sat me down on the floor in front of the long bank of back windows. "Here goes," he said. He went back to his bench and sat down facing me. Then he went to work.

He looked all around. He listened, not to anything I could hear, but to something inside him. With his eyes he made a wall between us. I saw him bring the other walls in closer to him, so he was in a smaller room filled with comfortable furniture. It was very quiet. Lucian seemed worn out. It was night. He wasn't quite alone—there was someone in a room off to his right—but he was the only one still awake. I could see all of this simply from his manner, even though most of it was new to me. It was remarkable.

Slowly he turned his eyes toward the receiver of the phone. He was looking less and less like Lucian. For one thing he was straight; this was somehow perfectly obvious. Whatever it was that had let me know he was gay in the first place was gone. His face, though still attractive, became ordinary and tired. He was sad, and confused, and had been hurt; it was late, he was cold. I took a last sip of my interesting tea and forgot about it altogether. In Lucian's head some argument was going on, something to do with the phone. He looked at it again, almost touched it, didn't quite touch it. The other person, the sleeping person, was on his mind again. Then gone. His hand rested on the phone. Abruptly, greedily, he lifted the receiver and punched a number, six digits, very fast, a familiar number. He hesitated. He moved away from the phone. He poked the seventh number.

"Catherine? It's me. I'm sorry to wake you at this hour, I . . ."

Catherine said something.

"I don't know, two, two-thirty, something like that. I know," he said in a rush, "I said I wasn't going to call, and believe me, I wasn't; I just didn't seem to have any choice, I had to call you."

The voice broke in again.

"Emily is sleeping," he answered. So, it was Emily in the other room. His voice dropped furtively, as if he feared saying her name might wake her.

Then the other party spoke to him.

"Well I'm sorry. Can you take it in the other room? I only need a minute," he pleaded. "Okay. Thanks."

There was a moment while Catherine left the phone to take it elsewhere, and Lucian's character was alone. He looked terrified. When Catherine picked up again it was as if she had breathed life into him through the phone. He said Hi. Then,

"I've been thinking. I know you've gotten used to us being broken up"—he spoke very slowly now—"and I've gotten used to us being broken up too. I really have. It's just that yesterday when we were all four in that elevator—" He looked up. I could see him fight the absurdity of this for an instant. "I couldn't help feeling—it was the strangest feeling—I couldn't help feeling like you and I were the only *real* people there. And the others, Emily and—right, Frank," he said, and he hated the work Frank which the voice at the other end of the line supplied for him; he took it into his mouth like a chunk of raw meat, "were characters or something, I don't know. Like—props."

Catherine spoke.

Lucian winced but went on resolutely, "Well did you feel anything like that?"

There was a horrible silence. It went on much too long after Catherine finished answering him.

"Oh, I was surprised to see you too, believe me," Lucian said, sounding very different now. A note of hysteria climbed through his voice with the deliberateness of a chromatic scale. "That was the longest elevator ride I ever took." He laughed. "I thought I was going to tear the railing out of the wall, did you see what I was doing? I was gripping it so hard; I wonder why they put those railings in elevators anyway. So you can hold on if the cable breaks? Something to hold onto while you slash to your death, that's convenient." His voice was less and less resonant, light, almost shrill, but he gripped the phone receiver in both hands as if it were the railing he mentioned. His knuckles and fingernails were white.

Catherine said something brief.

"No, I don't think Emily even knew what was happening. Oh, she knows that was you, I told her; she just doesn't know how hard it hit me. She's—very sweet. She's—nice. Kind."

Catherine spoke again.

"Yes. He looks kind," he agreed. There was a tiny pause. "You know," he suddenly went on, but in a tone like that of normal conversation, "I saw Leona last week, she's smoking again, I knew she wouldn't really quit—"

He broke off all of the sudden; Catherine had asked him something sharp.

"Well, I guess just to say hello," he answered, then immediately acknowledging the untruth and cowardice of this said, "and to let you know that I've been thinking about you—a lot, and—" from here on his words came harder and harder. He wasn't crying but he was struggling fearfully against it. His voice quivered wildly. "—And that I know we were awful together. And that . . . I know we were both unhappy. And—that I was thinking about you, and I wanted you to know, I *want* you to know—" he kept his tears in his eyes by tilting his head back at a strange angle—"if you ever—I know it isn't very likely—but if you ever needed someone to turn to, you could turn to me." He finished all in a rush. Still with both hands he put the receiver back into its cradle. Slowly he removed his hands from it, watching it through the tears that now fell along his cheeks. He seemed to think it might do something—jump, betray him. He remembered Emily, still asleep in the next room: he had been treacherous. But he had had to be. The scene ended. A moment later he looked straight at me. There were tears in my eyes.

We sat staring at each other. I think Lucian was just glad he'd reached me; he didn't say much of anything. After a while he asked me if I thought he did right to make the changes he had in the monologue. "Because the way we had it at first," he said, "it was more like he was sure the person he was speaking to was a terrible person. But it seemed like it would be better if he sort of had some feelings for the person too, you know? Like he's torn between them."

I nodded and agreed it was better. I kept remembering that first glance Lucian had shot me in the elevator at Helicon. He didn't miss much. And he was a very good actor.

TWELVE

꒰꒱

PATTY BATES COAXED out the unbuttoned left-hand cuff
of her black and forest-green silk shirt so that it stuck half
an inch out from under the left sleeve of her black cashmere
cardigan, laid her left wrist flat on her chrome and walnut
desk, made a fulcrum of her right elbow, raised her gold
Cross Executive ballpoint pen wrong end down in the pinch
of her right thumb and index finger, and with fell aim
speared the unoffending split of her buttonhole. Then,
sadly, she released both weapon and victim. The pen rolled
away, harmless. The cuff shrank again into its cashmere recess. Patty then delicately folded up her right earlobe and
stuffed it into her ear. "Melanie, I don't know," she said.

I was confused. "What's the big deal about?"

"Well, the songs you sent—"

"Yes?"

"I don't see how we can use them."

I felt a tiny warning shock; or maybe I just imagine I
did in retrospect. "Okay," I said, my first object being to
let her know this news was not going to kill me. "But what's
the problem? None of them's usable?"

"Um, they're just so—we don't feel they quite meet the

118

needs of any of our . . . the market," she mumbled, spinning her pen on its side and not looking at me.

I smiled, surprised, and even laughed a little. "Are they
bad?" I asked. "I didn't think they were bad—"

"Not *bad*," she broke in quickly, "not at all, I mean—
but just . . . so unusual," she finally breathed with relief.
She leaned forward on the last word and stretched her lips
around it exaggeratedly, then backed up again and looked
apologetic. "You know."

"But I don't know. Are they—is it because they're ballads?" I was madly recalling the best song I'd submitted,
mentally tearing through it to find what could possibly be
called unusual in it. The rhythm, the lyrics, the melody? I
couldn't find it. I reviewed another one, a third one. What?
They seemed fine to me; they seemed perfectly fine.

"No—"

"Because they're love songs? Is that—don't you think
love songs are still marketable?"

"It's not that," she said, making a gesture to stop me
from throwing out suggestions. Evidently she hadn't yet
been able to think of a way to explain this to me, though
she must have known this conversation was coming. Her
small pale forehead wrinkled as she looked at me again.
Then, "They're too personal," she said.

This was one accusation that had never been made against
my work before. I frowned. "Oh, well . . . I know they're
more personal than what I usually write, but they're no
more—personal than, say, what Van Morrison's always written. The lyrics, you mean?"

She nodded. "Mostly."

"They're not more personal—you mean idiosyncratic,
don't you?—not more than . . ." I searched for a name, dis-

carding several before I found one. Not Carly Simon, not James Taylor, not Carole King, not—well, maybe Phoebe Snow? Maybe— "Laura Nyro," I said. "Or—"

"Laura Nyro does her own stuff. So does Morrison."

"Joni Mitchell."

"Does her own stuff."

"Randy Newman."

"His own—"

"*Some* people do those people's stuff," I said.

"Years after the writer has recorded it first. It's a different kind of writing, a different kind of career from yours. Anyway, those people are not exactly shipping platinum these days. They're prestige artists left over from the sixties—"

I interrupted her. "Are you saying that because I've written something a little more personal than usual you won't even give me a chance with it? Disco is dead you know. Don't you want me to grow?"

"That's why I suggested the reggae angle—"

"I don't want an angle, I want—"

"Okay," she broke in, "tell me who you would like me to cast these songs for. You tell me. Who?"

I couldn't think of a name. "Wait, give me a minute. This isn't exactly my end of the business."

"It is when you bring in material like this. I can't think of a soul." She paused, then went on doubtfully, "I did think we might take 'Every Kind of Happiness' to—God, maybe even to Tina Holroyd, if we country it up a little—"

"No," I said without thinking. I didn't want it 'countried up.'

Patty shrugged. "Okay then. There probably are younger artists who might be willing to take a chance—"

I jumped in irritably, "Jesus, it's not like I handed you

waltzes. I mean, they aren't Gregorian chants."

"Melanie, I don't get it. I know we're not used to working together, and maybe it's my fault, but it seems to me you're talking like an amateur. You have a certain reputation now. People count on a certain consistency of style from you. That's your career. If I take these new songs around and they don't go, I'm going to have a tough time getting the next batch listened to. That's all. It's very simple. These songs are not what you've made a career for yourself writing." She stared at me as if daring me to disprove her words. The slight New York accent she always had had become increasingly pronounced as she talked. For the first time I understood how she'd managed to get where she was in the company. She really was tough, much tougher than I was. She tapped her pen on the desk for emphasis. "I'll tell you the truth, I called Dick Adair in L.A. just to be sure I wasn't completely off base. He agreed with me. There's no act these are right for. The words are not accessible—"

"Not accessible? What about 'Every Kind of Happiness,' what's so inaccessible about a woman saying she's found—"

"'Every Kind of Happiness' is the exception," she broke in, "as I said. In that case it's the bridge that throws it off. But the bridge could be rewritten—"

"It doesn't need rewriting. It's a beautiful bridge. What's the matter with it?"

"The rhythm change—"

"But don't you get it? That comes in from the words; in the bridge she's talking about how tense and crazy things used to be—"

"I *get* it, Melanie; I can't *use* it," Patty snapped, tossing her pen aside. "People don't like a song that switches beats in the middle. Why am I telling you this? You know. Look, I don't want to argue with you. I *like* these songs. I *like* them. But that's all they are, they're songs, you see. They're not—" she took a breath, then went ahead and spilled it: "product."

"Oh." I couldn't seem to say anything else. Struck dumb, I guess you call it.

"So we can take them around if you want, but there's not much point in it; and it might even be counterproductive. Right?"

I didn't answer. We sat in silence for as much as fifteen seconds. Then, "But look at the Talking Heads, for example," I said. "I mean, how accessible is that?"

"Melanie, again, you're discussing two completely different things. Those people do their own material, they—"

"But the public likes it, they buy it. There is a market—"

"The Talking Heads found their market. David Byrne created his market. He's earned the right to speak in his own voice," she blurted out.

"And I haven't?"

She shook her head.

"I don't have the right to be myself?"

"At the cost of marketability," she said, "no."

Again I could find nothing to say. After a while I felt like crying; but I didn't. Patty started to look apologetic again, which made me feel even crummier.

"So," she said nervously.

"So. What do you suggest I do with them?"

"Set them aside?" she said after a silence. "See how you feel about them in a month or two. You probably don't have the perspective now—"

I suddenly realized the tip of my nose was half numb

with cold. Patty's office was just as frigid as it had been the first time I'd visited her; I hadn't remembered to bring a sweater. I shivered. "I don't want perspective," I said suddenly. "I really don't. I like the songs."

"What do you want to do with them?"

I thought. "Write more like them."

"Okay. Fine," she said uncertainly. "There's no reason why you shouldn't try it. We don't want you to be unhappy. Follow it out."

"I think people will like them. I like them."

"Okay. Do you want me to take 'Every Kind of Happiness' to Tina—"

"No," I burst out unpleasantly. "I don't want you to do that. Listen, if what it takes to keep your songs whole around here is cutting them yourself maybe I'll just start doing that. How does that sound?" I'd had no idea I was going to say this. I sat looking defiantly at Patty anyway.

"You want to record?"

"Yes."

"I didn't know you were a performer."

"I'm not." I added inanely, "So, what do you think?"

"What can I think?" she asked. "If you want to be a performer, that's a big change."

"I know it's a big change. I'm not afraid. I've been in studios before, I know how they work—"

"Yes, but you can't just record though."

"What? Oh. Oh yeah."

"If you want to reach an audience you'll have to work live too. Play clubs. Go out on the road. People work for years to learn to be performers. You'd be starting very late."

"Yeah." I rubbed my bare arms, which were now freezing.

"Are you serious? You want to do this?"

"I don't know. Yes."

Patty shrugged unhappily. "Okay." She picked up her phone and hit three digits on the intercom. "Okay. Let's get Walter Preisler down here and we'll discuss it."

※

"So," I said to Lucian two hours later, having already recapped the above in the cab, "I'm going to do a showcase."

"How do you mean, a showcase?"

We were in a furniture store called Tandis Que, looking for a couch to buy in celebration of Lucian's having had his monologue videotaped. He'd been taping it while I was at my meeting, and thought the session had gone very well. The couch was his idea, of course, not to mention beginning the search at this tiny, outrageous shop. "You don't want to go to a department store. All you'll see there is trash," he'd said. "It'd just be a waste of time." Now he was floating at a fair clip up and down the store, his eyes narrowly focused, his expression calculating. When it came to buying things Lucian did not fool around. The saleswoman watched him approvingly. Her furniture had met its proper audience.

"You set up a gig in a small club where the publishers or whoever it is can see you work," I said, "and you do like a sampler. A short set, maybe six songs. So they can see how you do, how the audience likes you."

"You mean you're going to play in public?" He stopped drifting and turned to face me. The saleswoman frowned.

"Try not to sound shocked."

"Oh Melanie, that's wonderful."

"I don't know how wonderful it's going to be considering

I haven't worked in public since I can't remember when. I lied to Patty and Preisler. He's setting up the gig. I've never even worked solo, ever."

"But you can play. I've heard you."

"At home."

"So?" He'd started floating again and now suddenly leaned down close to the back of a sofa. "Look at this fabric—it's nice. I wonder if they have it in other colors."

"I'm sure they must. The point is, home is totally different: no sound system, no pressure, you don't need to have much of a voice—I know nothing at all about stage presence. I don't know how to put on a show."

"You don't need to put on a show," he said, sitting down on the sofa now under scrutiny. "God this is hard. You just be yourself."

"That's a foldout bed," said the saleswoman. "They're always hard. It's because of the frames."

"I'm going to have to practice an awful lot now. Being yourself is something you have to work for in a performance. I do know that."

"Yes . . . maybe. I know in acting—is this available without the foldout bed? We don't want a foldout bed, do we?"

Lucian had his own bed now, in his own bedroom. We'd bought it for him my second day back from Maine.

"No," I said.

"Yes," said the saleslady. "Any of these models can be ordered with or without a bed in it."

"Oh, that's good. Melanie—" Lucian cast off and resumed his drift, "I could coach you on how to perform, you know. I am an actor. I'm sure it's the same pretty much. Can this be done in another color? The same fabric?"

"Certainly. These are just models, so you can see the

shapes and sizes. I have thousands of fabrics you can have them covered with. You're interested in chairs as well, I imagine? How much did you wish to spend?"

I didn't think 'wish to spend' was a very accurate description of the state of things, and didn't answer her. I caught up to Lucian, who had seated himself in an oatmealy chair and was twirling an oatmealy ottoman. "If I screw up this showcase," I murmured to him, "I may be in a real funny situation for bread. I'm asking them to put some performing and recording provisions in my new contract—Pelion, that is. But if they don't like what they see at the showcase they're not going to be interested—"

"Would you like to look at some of the fabric books?" the saleswoman offered hopefully.

"No thank you," said Lucian. "What then? Would they cancel your whole contract? Melanie, this furniture is garbage," he whispered, leaning in to my ear. "A modular couch? I mean, *please.*"

"Then let's get out of here. No, not cancel it. They'd just offer me—I don't know what they'll offer me."

"You're going to knock them out, Melanie, I can feel it. I'll help you. I'll be a big help." The saleslady glared at our disappearing backs. "I'm so excited for you," said Lucian, suddenly throwing his arms around me and kissing me. "I *told* you you were an artist."

⚜

Many couches later we returned home to find Benjy Dennison camped on our doorstep. Seeing him and Lucian together gave me an odd jolt. Somehow I hadn't quite realized they inhabited the same planet.

Even more disconcerting was the discovery that I didn't

really care about seeing Benjy. I gave a little screech when I realized who it was, and ran up to hug him (we'd spotted him as we came down the block); but by the time I got to him I knew I didn't feel the kind of joyful surprise that had appeared to move me. In fact, I sort of resented his sudden materialization where he didn't belong. I'd never been sorry to see Benjy Dennison before, not once in my life. I should have known something very peculiar was up with me, but I didn't see it at the time.

Of course we all went inside. We took a bottle of cold wine down to the garden and sat around there drinking in the hot, heavy end of afternoon. Heat lightning trembled at the edges of the fading day. Benjy had his knapsack. As dusk fell and we talked I wondered privately where exactly he would spend the night.

"What happened to you? I got back to Webster and you weren't there," said Benjy, stretching out his legs and rubbing his knees as if they hurt. He always looked as if he couldn't quite get enough room to stretch out in. "I gather you had a run-in with your mom?"

"Rather."

"Still pissed?"

I dropped my head into my hands and thought a moment. "Not especially." I looked up again to find him smiling sympathetically into my eyes.

"She can't help it," he said.

"True."

"So," he said.

"So."

We took sips from our wine to have something to do. Lucian was watching us attentively, as if to learn something from us. A bank of clouds rolled in from the east and the whole sky slowly darkened. "Your mother must be a very strong woman," Lucian said.

"In her fashion."

"The wedding's still on though," Benjy volunteered. "That's a good sign." He kept flashing uncertain glances over toward Lucian, followed by inquisitive ones at me. He seemed to be waiting for me to tell him who Lucian was. "Are you coming?"

"You bet. When is it?"

"You mean nobody's told you?"

"Communication breakdown. You know. My family."

"It's the nineteenth."

"Of September?"

"Uh-huh."

"Oh shit. My showcase is the seventeenth. I guess I can make it."

"I want to go too," Lucian suddenly said.

"To the showcase?"

"To the wedding. Of course I'm going to the showcase. I'm your teacher," he added, with a smile of pride. The clouds were multiplying so quickly I could hardly make out the smile. I got up to switch the floodlight on. "I'm going to teach Melanie how to perform," he added.

Returning, I explained to Benjy the new veering of my career. "What do you think?" I grinned. "Do I look like a star?"

"Uh-huh. Like a Jewish star."

"What's that supposed to mean?"

He only laughed. "Are you a musician too?"

"Lucian's an actor. Benjy deals drugs," I said informatively. "He can afford to laugh at us artists because his life is firmly rooted in the respectable soil of commerce. Right? A man of affairs."

Benjy nodded.

"By the way, how'd that run to Houston go?" I asked blandly.

"Okay," he said. I stared at him. His fine hair shone dully under the harsh white light, and his eyes glittered. "Oh, horrible," he laughed, giving up. "Another disaster. That's why I'm in New York—to salvage what I can. By the way, I called Jules just now, to get your address. He said you were living with a Twinkie. What's a Twinkie?"

"Oh Benjy," I sputtered despairingly. I hardly dared to look at Lucian. When I did I found his expression completely tranquil. He didn't pay much attention to Jules's opinions. He thought Jules was half in the closet himself. Benjy looked frankly bewildered. "It's nothing," I said. "Jules doesn't like Lucian."

"Oh, are you living here?" he asked, surprised.

Lucian nodded. Benjy looked questions at me.

"It's not—" I started, and stopped. "Oh hell. Let's go eat."

Benjy lit up some hash and we smoked it. As we walked the two blocks to one of the neighborhood pizza joints a cold rain suddenly overtook us. "You guys don't know what this means to me," I shouted as we ran, jackets over our heads, for the restaurant door. "Rain in the summer . . . Jesus I missed this!" By the time we'd finished dinner water was pouring down in vast uneven sheets that smashed against the pavement with a wet roar. I sprinted home through it in a state of bliss and arrived there drenched and freezing. We all did. Still, after all those years in California, to me being soaked it was a welcome inconvenience. Benjy had clothes in his pack so we all dried off and changed. Then Benjy and I rendezvoused in the living room, where the storm vigorously pelted the windows. After a while Lucian came upstairs too, dressed to go bar-hopping, a thin cane-handled umbrella under his arm.

"I'm going to visit a friend," he announced, standing by the door and balancing his linen jacket on the tip of an outstretched finger. His hair was still damp. He'd been looking at me oddly all evening; I had the idea he found something rather distasteful and vulgar in the thought that I might want to go to bed with Benjy. That we'd been lovers I had no doubt he picked up very fast, though there was no overt display between us. Now he held my eyes with his and added deliberately, "I may not be back tonight."

"Oh no," I said at once. "Don't feel you have to—I mean, just do what you like."

Benjy looked in puzzled silence from Lucian's face to mine. Lucian hesitated a moment longer as if weighing what I'd said. "All right," he concluded. "I'll do what I like."

The rain notwithstanding, he didn't come home till five. His absence was quite unnecessary: I couldn't seem to get interested in fooling around with Benjy anyway. Despite the vague affection I did (I'm relieved to say) still feel for him, my thoughts were all with Lucian. I hadn't realized till then what it meant to me to spend time with Lucian. Alone. Receiving his full attention. The ambiguity of our relationship had hardly troubled me till Benjy's visit pointed it up. Somehow I'd let this scarcely familiar person, whose bond to me had no name and no advocate, become important to my happiness. I was very concerned at his having gone out to leave Benjy and me alone. What did he think of my having a lover? Did it disgust him? There had been a cool purity in his manner that night that seemed to imply *he* would never betray me by showing an attachment to somebody else. Or perhaps I imagined this. The fact that I'd been writing love songs connected with Lucian jumped suddenly, painfully, embarrassingly into high relief; and the idea that I might be changing my career, taking risks with it, *to please him*, slowly began to take shape in that wordless inner chaos where knowledge starts.

Benjy was too discreet, and probably too high as well, to ask questions. Left alone, he simply swooped down on me. His mouth on mine aroused nothing in me. I kissed back negligently. He tried my cheek, then my neck and shoulders.

"I'm sorry," I finally said, embarrassed. "I can't seem to—do it—"

Benjy gestured toward the door. "That guy's not your boyfriend, is he?"

"No, nothing like that." I smiled at him ruefully, detaching myself from him and moving a little away. We sat on the floor in the living room listening to the rain. He put his hand in mine. I stared at it. "I don't know what's wrong with me," I said helplessly.

"You seem like you're maybe in love with someone."

"Oh no," I said, "that couldn't be."

He shrugged affably, putting his hand to my cheek for a moment, then dropping it and drawing back. "Just the wrong night then," he said.

"Oh yes," I said gratefully. He didn't kiss me again. I insisted on sharing my bed with him when he asked if he could crash somewhere, but only because by then we both knew it was only a question of sleeping.

"Something's happened to you," he said, without malice or mockery, just as he fell off to sleep. I lay awake beside him for hours. The storm moved away about four-thirty.

When Lucian came in I sneaked out to kiss him good-night.
Benjy took off in the morning.

⚹

The fact that Jules had called Lucian a Twinkie turned
out to our advantage. I used it the following day as a lever
to pry the next favor out of him. "It's just like Benjy Dennison to run straight from me to you and drop that. Like a
dog with a slipper," he muttered into the phone. I'd reached
him at the *Beat* again. "Boy, you really know how to pick
your friends."

"Your friends aren't such gems either," I said, thinking
of one in particular who'd just been busted for faking a na-
tional news story.

"At least they work for a living."

"Maybe. Anyway I'm glad you brought up the subject,
because work is what Lucian wants. Do you think you could
call—"

"An agent," he cut in gloomily. "Yes, okay. I give up."

"He got his tape made. It looks good. I'll be your best
friend for this, Jules."

"Swell."

"Only make it a really top agent, okay?"

"Theatrical?"

"Yes please."

"All right. I think I know someone. Don't get your hopes
up though."

"God love you."

"It may be a while before she can see him. She's in Lon-
don this week."

"She?"

"What's the matter, your boy afraid of women?"

"Oh Jules," I said, my temper slipping. "I'm going to hang up now. Thanks for this, really."

"Right."

The agent, whose name was Joan Dunbar, was out of town till the tenth. By the time she got back the first appointment she could give Lucian was the eighteenth. This was the day we'd been planning to fly up to Maine for Donald and Sharon's wedding. It was too good an opportunity to postpone, however; apparently there was a major off-Broadway production she'd been asked by Lionel Smith, the director, to help cast. Jules knew the play and grudgingly parted with the information that there might be a role in it just right for Lucian. The second lead, the female protagonist's brother. By this time the videotape had been processed and I'd played it over at the *Beat* office for Jules one day. He couldn't deny Lucian's talent: Jules really does love theater—it's one thing about him that's perfectly genuine—and Lucian's performance was dead on target. Jules guessed I had helped with the writing and continued to deprecate Lucian on this ground; he also guessed I was footing the bill, and dwelt on my fatuousness for a while; but in the end the stark ability and authority of Lucian's work excited him.

"I'll make sure Joan sees him herself," he told me, trying not to show his interest. "Thank God he isn't a loser."

We sent the tape over to her office ahead of time on Jules's advice. As far as the trip to Maine went, I changed Lucian's reservation to a flight that left the following morning. I'd go alone on the eighteenth and he'd come up the day of the wedding. It was scheduled to start at two-thirty P.M.

Right about this time is when Lucian heard Martin Ivory had a new lover living with him. Some well-wisher he ran into told him this, and that the new man's name was Gary, that he was an actor too, and that Ivory seemed very happy. Lucian wouldn't discuss the news, except to pass it along to me. He said it didn't matter since he was finished with Ivory anyhow; but later that night I walked into his room and found him sitting cross-legged on his bed, blowing his nose. His eyes were red, his cheeks wet. He jumped up, startled. He thrust the tissue he'd been using behind him as if it were guilty evidence. His embarrassment was such that I almost walked right out again. But I caught myself and asked if he was all right.

"I'm all right," he said, looking away, half-covering his eyes with his hand.

"Do you want to talk about it?"

"No thanks. I'd just—rather be alone, if it's okay."

I lingered in the doorway another moment: he looked so miserable. But then I said Okay and went upstairs. I'd have liked to help him; I was even a little hurt that he didn't want to talk to me. By the time he came up to kiss me good-night he seemed to have recovered his composure. He apologized for sending me away earlier.

"It's just something I have to work through on my own," he said. "You know what I mean? It's just old feelings."

"Whatever you want. You know where I am if you change your mind."

I let it go at that. I was busy myself those days.

I'd been working like crazy trying to get my showcase ready. I'd finally settled on five songs, with good old "Real Life" semiprepared and up my sleeve as an encore in case such a thing was needed. Actually the whole performance was pretty semiprepared; there just wasn't time to do it thoroughly. Besides "Every Kind of Happiness" and "If It's

Only Me"—which at least were ballads and needed a minimum of arranging—I was rehearsing three songs Helicon had never heard. One was a very upbeat tune, manic and driving, that came to me right after Benjy's visit; this was called "Those Are the Breaks" and had a lot of chug-chug sounds, like a train, in the chorus, and a beat of dead silence at the end of every eighth bar. Kind of silly, but exuberant and fun to sing. The fourth was a blues tune I never bothered to take to them, though I'd written it years before. It was called "The Easy Way Out" and I wrote it as a kind of joke for my then boyfriend (a bass guitarist who wore snakeskin boots and a cape on stage) to break the tension between us during a prolonged standoff. The fifth song was one I wrote for Iris right after she died. It's called "Someone To Sing To." I'd never played it for anyone. The first time I did was for Lucian.

He really did coach me as he'd promised, partly I think because it was better to keep busy than to sit around wondering how Ivory and Gary were getting along. Less is more was his major dictum. We decided that just as the key to acting is listening, the key to singing is telling. I told my songs, straight and simple; that was all. That was enough. I wasn't adept at getting in touch with my feelings, let alone expressing them out loud, least of all in a public place. With all eyes on me. Mike technique, the hazy blind of a spotlight, the sounds an audience makes while you're playing—all these things had to be learned, anticipated, gotten used to. One afternoon in the living room Lucian brought up the business of makeup and costume. We had a rather difficult hour apropos of this.

"I think you should just play up your strong points and never mind about working for an image," he said.

"My strong points?" I asked. "And what would they be?"

He seemed surprised. "Well, your height, for one, and your . . . angularity—"

"That's a strong point?" I asked, immediately annoyed at myself for having interrupted this interesting line of thought.

"Yes, sure. It's very dramatic—you have a very dramatic look."

I restrained myself from contradicting him. "And what else?"

"Your eyes," he said promptly. "They're your strongest feature of all."

"Uh-huh. And—?"

"Well, that's it I guess," he said, looking me over impartially. "Those are the main points to stress."

Tears rushed irresistibly to my favored eyes. I looked away; but to my horror one splashed down onto my arm.

"What's the matter?" he asked, quite sincerely taken aback.

"I don't," I swallowed to keep my voice steady, "like my looks."

"Why not?" All innocent surprise.

I shook my head, unable to speak for fear of sobbing. This was awful; I was utterly out of control. I felt helpless in a way I hadn't since childhood, as if the tears had been a river that carried me backwards in time. I relied completely on Lucian; I had to. It was dreadful.

"But Melanie, you're so pretty," he said.

I sobbed once and caught myself, choking the next one back. I shook my head miserably, still looking at the floor, and said "No." I started to laugh at his gallantry but as soon as the noises came out it turned into crying, all by itself, and there was nothing I could do: I just sat gasping and sobbing with my head bent down to my knees while Lucian looked on in amazement—or perhaps not amazement. At last he came over and knelt beside me, putting his hands on my shoulders, both hands, gently, stroking me, leaning over my bent back. He brought his head down next to mine and kissed my ear and my cheek. His arms went around me. I still looked away at the floor. I imagined how I must appear now, with my eyes swollen and red. The thing was hopeless, hopeless. He pitied me. I was abject.

"Melanie, I think you're *pretty*."

I said thank you. I stopped sobbing.

"It's the truth."

Immobile, I became aware of his arms encircling me. Pleasure and humiliation welled up together inside me. I shuddered. I said faintly, "It isn't."

"It is," He laughed—not a really good sign in Lucian. He was becoming embarrassed. I made a movement as if I were cramped in his embrace, thus giving him an excuse to free me and sit up himself. He did at once.

"I better go wash my face," I said, not looking at him. I stood up, still shaky, and stumbled away to the kitchen to bathe my eyes. After this we never discussed my so-called prettiness again. I put together an outfit to wear on stage and altered it bit by bit according to his suggestions. My showcase was not far away. I was doing every open-mike night I could, all over town, as well as rehearsing at home four or five hours a day. Jules helped me get half an hour on stage at the Front Door one night, after the regular show was over. Audiences seemed to respond to me readily and I was gradually gaining confidence. Lucian lectured me daily on centering my energy. We argued some about the audience and how I should connect with them. I think he some-times forgot this was singing, not acting. And then, all too soon, it was September 17. I had to go on stage at Xeno's, alone, at eleven P.M, ready or not.

THIRTEEN

❧❦

I HAD ALREADY changed into my performing clothes and was putting on and taking off my makeup for the third time when I happened to catch Lucian cruising past the bathroom. "But where are you going?" I followed him up the staircase and into the living room, a mascara-blackened cotton ball still in my hand. "It's almost nine-fifteen."

"Have you seen my—oh, here it is." He took his wallet from on top of the piano and shoved it into his back pocket. "I'll be right back."

"Don't be 'right back.' Don't go," I said, feeling frantic. "Why are you going now? I need you to be with me."

"I'm coming right back," he repeated. "I'm going to get a surprise for you."

"I don't want a surprise," I said. "If you're not at the club when I go on tonight I'll have fits. I want you to stay here, okay?"

He blew me a theatrical kiss.

"Oh Lucian, please don't. You're always late—"

He was gone.

Jules showed up at nine-thirty to ride with me to the club. Jules had been practically human toward me lately.

It seemed his determination to run me out of town was fading. Probably he just got used to the idea of having me around. "Where's young Olivier?"

"He went out to get a surprise for me."

Half an hour later Jules said, "Surprise! No Lucian. What do you want to do?"

"Let me write him a note," I muttered, and did so, reminding him where the club was and what time I went on. I left it in the middle of the living room floor.

"Nice guy," observed Jules as we looked for a taxi.

Jess, the owner of Xeno's, was a sociable type who managed the place himself and took a personal—you might say mildly intrusive—interest in the careers of the entertainers who performed there. He and I had been introduced several times by common acquaintances, and he greeted me that night with a hail-fellow-well-metness that I could have done without. His hands were warm and puffy and he held mine in them longer than was either necessary or desirable, coyly asking whether Jules Armour was my husband or my brother. I escaped, on the pretext of nerves, into the dressing room.

This was a dingy little hole with a mirror along one wall and a counter running below it to make a kind of vanity table. The counter was thickly spread with the debris of performers past: spilled powder, burnt matches, empty lipsticks, half a plastic tampon case, a Bic pen with all the ink gone, guitar picks, someone's capo, cigarette ashes . . . I had a good chance to look it over while I hid there. Jules said Break a leg, shook my hand, and went to get a table. After a while I raised my eyes and made myself look in the dusty mirror. It was ten-forty-five and Lucian was still missing.

"Who are you?" I inquired in passing of the image in the mirror. A knock sounded on the hollow door. I jumped up.

"Just me," said Patty Bates, coming in. "Are you nervous? You look great."

She stood gazing at me as I imagine sorority sisters gaze at one another in moments of pleasant crisis. I suddenly felt sorry for both of us. "Not too nervous, thanks." I dropped into the only chair in the room and looked up at her. My hands went wet.

"Walt Preisler's out in front," she said, leaning against the counter, "and Tony Paressi, do you know him? He's in A and R at Pelion."

"No."

"Well you'll meet him after the show," she said. "We'll go next door for a drink, okay? It'll give us a chance to talk."

"Okay," I said distractedly.

"I'd like you to meet him anyway. He's a very talented guy. Good ear. He's starting to do some producing now."

"Uh-huh."

There was a longish pause during which I suppose Patty realized I was preoccupied. She stood up straight, reaching out for my cold, damp hand. "Good luck. I'll just . . . let you get ready." She left. A thin chalky streak ran across the back of her pleated skirt where she'd leaned up against the powdery counter. The place was really a mess. In a moment Jess knocked and came in, insisting on giving me a kiss for luck.

"I'm going to announce you in a minute," he said. "Come on."

"Please don't mention any of my old titles, will you?" I

trotted after him down the narrow hall. He motioned to me to keep my voice down. The man on stage, a stand-up comic, was just finishing. "Just say I'm a songwriter, okay?" I whispered.

He frowned. "Are you sure?"

"Yes." On stage the comic delivered his closing line and started to say his good-nights.

"That's a mistake," Jess said, shaking his head disapprovingly as the club broke out in applause. There was a pretty fair crowd. The comic suddenly shot past us like a runner just through the finish tape. His face was pale and covered with sweat.

"Just do it," I said.

He shrugged. "It's your funeral," he said cheerfully. He jumped onto the stage to do his emcee shtick, give people time to order drinks, clown for them a little. I looked around for the comic. He'd disappeared. There was an interesting smell of sweat and dust in the air. I wondered why I had worn the shirt I was wearing. I wondered how I was going to play when my hands were wet and frigid. My knees started to feel trembly. Was it Xeno's piano that had a chipped high C or the one at the Front Door? I couldn't even recall which way it faced. And where was Lucian? That question buzzed continually behind all the other questions. I wanted him with me. Had he come in at the last minute? Would he come backstage or just take a seat? I heard my name called and hopped onto the stage.

Miraculously, my panic evaporated completely the moment I reached the piano. It vanished smoothly and simply, like a theatrical scrim lifting after the ballet's overture. The bright lights, far from disturbing me, gave me a pleasant sense of disorientation and security both together. Their warmth felt like friendly hands. Seen but unseeing, I was alone and yet not alone. This was my moment. These people wanted to like me. The child in me came out—that infant whose every garbled word incites a riot of delight—and I began to heat up like the filament in a light bulb.

I sat down, all smiles, unselfconscious, and rolled into the intro to "Every Kind of Happiness." The mike was set up so that I could cheat out and sing almost directly toward the audience. This was not the piano with the chipped C, I found, but it did have a noisy pedal I had somehow overlooked when I'd come to check it out that afternoon. Lucian and I had decided I should say nothing till I'd played my first number. That had seemed like a good idea, clean and dramatic, but now that I was there it felt very odd to vault right into the thing. All very well for Lucian to have ideas: he probably wasn't even here. I shoved him out of my thoughts. The intro was nearly done. I had to sing.

I think I'd better mention here what a very strange voice I have. It isn't like other people's. I got a little training once from a vocal coach I used to go out with, and when we discovered where my natural register lay we were both astonished. It's a whole octave below my speaking voice, a deep, rumbly, croaky growl I'd never known was there till he unearthed it. For some reason I kept remembering Walter Preisler was out in the audience. What would he think when he heard my voice? Of all my many shortcomings as a performer I thought my voice the most damning. If he attacked it I could submit no defense. I could hardly open my mouth for fear. When at last I did my vocal cords refused to come together and all I came up with was air—no tone, no resonance. The whole first verse sounded like someone making a deathbed confession.

It was so awful I laughed. This was the best thing I did all night, not least because it relaxed my throat. I coughed, announced determinedly, "I *said*," and went back to the first verse again. This time I sang it right and gratefully. I knew at once the room was with me. It was a wonderful feeling, that connectedness. As if a perfect understanding existed between me and these apparent strangers, the kind of sympathy true lovers reputedly have, the kind that obviates speech. I'd never felt it before. I found myself looking into the lights trustfully, as if into a roomful of friends assembled for no other purpose than to commune with me. I was high.

The next song was "Those Are the Breaks." People got behind it so fast they were clapping in rhythm from the first chorus. I didn't have the heart to go straight to "Someone To Sing To" after that—it's a sad song, and everyone was feeling so good—so I jumped ahead and did "Easy Way Out" first. I was getting all kinds of shouts and whoops during the chorus, and by the time I hit the second verse I was flying:

> You say you saw me at the Roxy
> Making eyes at all the boys
> I guess I got a little rowdy
> And I made a little noise
> I had my high heels on
> I wore a red satin dress
> You want to know what I was doing?
> Honey, can't you guess?
> I was looking for the easy way out . . .

And so on. "I think you know what I'm talking about /

Talking about the easy way, easy way out." Bam.

Then "Someone to Sing To." Taking the mood down so far so fast was not easy to do and I didn't entirely succeed. I made the mistake of listening to my own voice for a while, and so lost half the song and maybe half the audience. I couldn't get a fix on where they were until maybe midway through "If It's Only Me"; then I knew they were with me again. I said hardly anything between the tunes; just hello and how were they and how I was. "If It's Only Me" is one of those Ignorance is Bliss songs—don't tell me if I'm the only one who cares about this relationship because I'd rather go on making a jerk of myself and having fun—apparently they could relate. The applause (which I was mainly too busy to listen to, and which didn't interest me too much anyway) doubled when I stood up to leave. Jess appeared at the edge of the stage and told me to take an encore.

Gratified, I sat down again and launched into "Real Life." That's where I made my mistake, I guess, though I didn't know it till later. At the time I was just blown away by how well it went. Gloria Mack's voice to mine is Hyperion to a satyr and then some, but the audience responded anyway and some people even got up and danced between the tables. That gave me a charge, seeing people move to my tune, my music. When I was done I split from the stage quick like a bunny.

My hands were still cold and it seemed as if the sweat had been absorbed back into them, my fingers were so stiff. My chest was covered with perspiration, my mind raced, and for hours afterward I could feel the different muscles of my legs twitch and jerk and slowly, slowly relax. On stage I hadn't been aware of any of this; now my body insisted on some attention. I hurried to the dressing room flexing my hands. Jules was there before I was. The next performer, a raw-boned, blond singer-songwriter, was there too, sitting in the chair and smoking a joint with his eyes closed. Jules shook my hand again.

"You did good, kid." For him this is an effusion. "What did you think?"

Jess's voice and the audience's laughter dimly penetrated the walls. I asked, "Where's Lucian?"

Jules shrugged.

I looked around as if he might have been hiding under the vanity counter. "Did you see him outside?"

"Didn't see anybody." Jules was watching me with the hawkeyes he got from my mother.

"Shit." I found myself eyeing the doorway narrowly. I wanted to wait here a minute longer in case Lucian might still appear.

"What's next?"

The man in the chair suddenly spoke, moving only his lips. "Want a hit?"

It was unclear to whom he addressed himself. He opened his eyes just enough for me to see they were brown, but they weren't focused on anything. "No thanks," I said.

"Do you have to do anything here?" Jules asked me.

"Hit?" said the singer, this time slightly turning his wrist so that the joint in his hand pointed toward Jules.

"No thank you. Melanie answer me, what are you supposed to do now, anything?"

"I have to find Patty. The woman from Helicon."

The singer erupted, emitting a long, swift stream of smoke. "You got someone from Helicon here?"

"Uh-huh."

"They're a good outfit, big outfit. Came just to see you?"

"Yes."

"Who are you?"

I looked at Jules. "I'm his sister."

The singer tilted his head back so he could look at me from under his heavy eyelids. "See if you can get them to stay here for my set, will you? I'm on in ten minutes. Okay?"

Jules was already at the door. "Yeah, I don't know if I can, man," I said. "I'll see what I can do."

"Thanks a lot. You're an all right lady, you know?"

I despaired of Lucian's coming. We hurried out.

"Really all right, man."

Jules and I shook our Armours-can't-imagine-how-these-people-survive headshake at each other and exchanged the sooner-we're-gone-the-better glances as we went down the corridor. Midway down the hall, in front of a fire exit, Patty intercepted us. Smiling, she put out her hands as if to hug me; but her elbows were so close to her sides a hug was out of the question. I thought of kissing her cheek and waved at her instead. "How's it going?"

"Melanie, I loved your performance," she said enthusiastically. "I really did."

I took this in while introducing her to my brother.

"I'm so glad to meet you. You'll come with us, won't you?"

"Oh drinks," I said suddenly.

"What?"

"I just remembered we're supposed to have drinks."

"Well yes, I want you to meet Tony and everything. Come on, they're waiting out front. Will you come Jules?"

"Mm Patty," I said, trying wildly to reckon exactly how stupid a thing I was doing, "I wonder if I could . . . skip the drinks."

"Hmm?"

"I just—" I shot a glance at Jules, then looked away at once. "I can't seem to—for some reason, I guess the performance and all, I just feel so dead tired I don't know how I'll hold my head up." I gave a short, false laugh. The button eyes in Patty's tiny face shone anxiously. "You think I could meet him tomorrow? Tony, I mean."

"I don't know about tomorrow, but sometime, I'm sure—" she said, sounding very unsure. "Are you really— well of course if you're tired . . ."

"You'll perk up in a minute—" Jules began, glaring at me. He knew exactly what was going on.

"No, I'm really exhausted," I cut him off. "Would you just tell them I can't come? I'm sorry."

Reluctantly she acceded. "At least come and meet him," she said at last. "You can say hi to Walt, too."

We did this, out in the warm, close evening on the sidewalk in front of Xeno's. Tony Paressi was a slickly handsome Englishman with a well-clipped beard and what's usually called a great haircut. He was obviously delighted not to have to sit and chat with me. "A shame," he said, fixing my eyes with his and shaking my hand with one of those warm solid grips that people who point out how upfront they are use. "You're not accustomed to performing, that's what it is."

"Very likely." I kept trying to look, in spite of myself, into the door of the club.

"Very glad I could make it tonight though," he went on. There was a pause before he added, "You're a talented girl."

"I'm pleased you think so."

"We'll talk," he concluded, with a final powerful glance, the kind Superman uses to cut holes in doors. Then he turned away and resumed a discussion with Walter Preisler.

I pushed Jules into a taxi. "What'd you do that for?" he asked.

"Do what?"

"Duck out on the drinks. You dope, that's the whole point of these things. You have to play the game offstage with them."

"I know that."

"Then why don't you do it?"

"He doesn't want to work with me anyway, couldn't you see that?"

"Who doesn't?"

"Tony."

He'd seen it all right. But, "That's not the point," he said. "If it's not Tony it could be someone else at Pelion. Maybe he knows a producer who's looking for someone—"

"Look, could you stop arguing with me? I'm feeling peculiar enough as it is."

"You didn't even meet Tony before you begged off," he pointed out. "Back in the hallway you said you couldn't come. What for, Melanie? What does that Twinkie mean to you?"

"If you know why I wanted to leave, why are you grilling me about it?"

"I'm not grilling you, I'm trying to understand what your life is about."

The cab jolted angrily over a pothole. Hot night air, damp and heavy, swept across us. We had one of those old-fashioned taxis with jump seats, and a Turkish cabbie I think, Kemal Somebody.

I moved away from Jules so that the yaw of the cab could not possibly throw us together. "My life is not 'about' anything. What do you mean? It's my life, that's all. I'm trying to get used to living here, okay? I like being with Lucian. I don't notice you calling me up every night to see how I am." I paused. "I'm trying to open my career up a little. I hope. Is that okay?"

"When you skip out on a crucial business meeting on account of you can't wait half an hour to see some faggot, your life is not okay."

"He isn't a faggot," I spat out furiously.

"He isn't?"

"I meant to say," I corrected, my face immediately burning with a climbing flush, "it wasn't a crucial meeting. It's all right. I'll meet with him tomorrow."

"You're going to Maine tomorrow."

"I'll meet with him next week then. It's not a big deal. I did well. Why don't you let me enjoy that?" We stopped for a light. I stared at a green Bulova watch sign, listening to the click of the meter, savagely willing my crimson blush to settle.

"Melanie."

"What."

"I'm not trying to take that away from you. It just makes me angry to see you turning backflips for a," he caught himself, "a teenager. Okay? I'd like to know what you're getting from him that's so wonderful you don't mind risking your career for him. He didn't even show up tonight."

"No kidding." These words came out on a quiver of breath; the instant I opened my mouth to say them the tears that had been collecting in my eyes spilled over and splashed down my cheeks. I turned my face away toward the night and the speeding row of streetlamps.

"Well, so why do you worry about him?"

I shook my head and covered my eyes with one hand,

rubbing them hard, then my forehead and cheeks.

"Do you love him?" he asked. "Are you in love with him?"

I hiccuped, meaning to laugh. "How could I be in love with him? He doesn't even like girls."

"You're sure?"

I glanced up, astonished Jules was willing even to ask this question. "This is stupid, Jules. Yeah, I'm sure. Fairly sure."

He said deliberately, "Maybe you better find out for perfectly sure."

In the dim muggy night glare Jule's face hovered before me, a delicate blue. I looked into it carefully. For once he had stopped looking put-upon. He wasn't even laughing at me.

I couldn't seem to answer him out loud. After a while I sniffled wetly. "Do you have a tissue?" I asked finally, for something to say.

He reached for a back pocket.

"Never mind. I do." I blew my nose for a while under the rattle and grind of the cab. Hope began to take root like a weed in my heart, spreading in all directions. Maybe Lucian did love me. Really. He said he loved me. He acted that way. He had followed me home, left Ivory, moved in. He never went out at night without me. He didn't have sex with me, but I didn't think he had it with anyone else. Maybe he did love me. Because all of the sudden I knew I loved him. Thoroughly loved him. As a friend, and more than a friend. I wanted him for my lover—my constant lover, my true lover. It wasn't a question of sexual union. It was more than that, or other than that. The knowledge that had begun the night Benjy visited me in New York had at last surfaced fully. I wanted to build a life with Lucian. Why couldn't we? If I told him how I felt, what might he not confess in return? Till tonight I had never named my emotion, to him, to Jules, or even to myself. Now a tenderness so sweet it seemed more a visiting spirit than a native feeling swept through me. It throbbed all around me like an aura. I was afraid Jules would see it; but he only said goodnight as usual when the cab dropped me in front of my house. I thanked him absently, leaving him to pay the whole fare himself, and ran up the steps to the door. I fumbled for my key, then found that the handle turned: it was unlocked. Good. Then Lucian was home and all right. Wherever he'd been, whatever had happened, however he'd managed to miss my showcase, I didn't care. I wouldn't ask. I just wanted to see him. I wanted to speak to him. He wasn't upstairs, but the note I had left on the floor for him was gone. I ran down, my whole body trembling with new love and this wild desire to tell it. He wasn't in his bedroom. He wasn't in mine. I found him finally in the garden, safe, a glass of wine in his hand, his back to the sliding door —which stood open to admit the night—leaning his bright, graceful head against the curving shoulder of Martin Ivory.

FOURTEEN

❧

THERE WAS SOMETHING all too familiar about the next few minutes. Lucian heard me coming and jumped up, waylaying me at the door. The pure hurt of finding what I had found in the garden scarcely announced itself to me before a chorus of inner voices rose to drown it out with an ancient drone: How had I dared to hope? Why was I still such an idiot? I'd gotten no more than I deserved, imagining good could come of this. How could I have imagined my love would be returned? And more. This sharp self-castigation was more tolerable to me than the blow that occasioned it. I was in rueful but nonetheless effective command of myself before Lucian even finished his explanation: it was all coincidence; he'd gone out to get roses for me and there on the street at a café next door to the florist's, there sat Ivory. He couldn't pretend not to see him; one thing had led to another—a drink, an admission on Ivory's part that he wasn't happy—after a while Lucian realized he had to give him a chance to talk, at least, for old time's sake if nothing else. He apologized for having missed the show—though it wasn't his fault, Ivory wouldn't let him leave—

"Are you going back to him?" I broke in rudely, gluttonously anxious to know the worst at once.

He looked surprised. "Oh no, nothing like that. No. It was just—he needed to talk. He's in a bad way," he added, dropping his voice. All this time Ivory had been sitting on the patio, his back to us, politely not noticing I was there until I was ready to meet him. "I feel kind of sorry for him, you know?"

Now the weed hope began to foliate again. I thought, "I must feel sorry for Ivory too, at all costs. The power he has is in the importance I give him." I determined to annihilate him with pity, and summoning up all my little store of condescension I went outside.

He stood as I walked out and around him. The floodlight was on. He was a tall, rangy man, with long thin bones and skin that had tanned and faded many times. I'd have taken him for thirty sooner than forty. His worn eyes, green and suffering, made in that first instant absolutely no answer to the dare in mine. He had already surrendered. He was wretched. His soft, long, handsome mouth barely managed a smile.

I said hello.

I'd been expecting, from Lucian's savage reports of him, a vulgar, callous, balding semihoodlum. The gentle hand that slipped so gratefully into mine rested there an extra moment because mine was the hand that now held Lucian's. "You must be Melanie," he said.

I smiled and sat down rather abruptly. He sat too. Lucian couldn't make up his mind where to settle; after considerable looking around he picked a spot just between us but some distance away, so that the three of us made an isosceles triangle with Lucian at the apex.

Ivory spoke in a quiet, lilting patter, so that you continually listened to make out what kind of an accent he had.
It was very attractive, and I imagine deliberately cultivated.
"I'm glad to meet you," he went on. "I understand you're
a singer." He started to regain what I suppose was his normal social presence. The wounded look in his eyes disappeared and was replaced by the beginnings of a kind of
shrewd curiosity about me. I've seen that look in the eyes
of other people, unconventional but successful businessmen
mostly. As its object one is at first flattered, then gradually
but increasingly thrown off balance.

"Not really a singer," I answered vaguely.

"Lucian, why don't you get Melanie a wine glass?" he
said, about to take a sip from his own. The bottle sat per-
spiring between us.

Lucian started to move automatically, then stopped to
glare at Ivory. "Get it yourself," he told him.

"This is your place, Luke," Ivory said, laughing. He
seemed all at once to relax.

I said quickly, "I don't want any, thanks."

"How did your show go tonight?"

"I told Ivory about it," Lucian explained. "God I wish
I'd been there."

"Never mind." This was purely for Ivory's benefit. The
vulnerability he'd displayed in the first moment of our meeting had disappeared altogether. Now he watched me carefully, trying I think to gauge what power, if any, I held over
Lucian. I felt I was in over my head, and floundered. "It
went fine. Really fine, in fact."

"Did the people from Helicon offer you a recording contract?" Lucian asked, with a proud glance sidelong at Ivory.

"It doesn't happen that fast," I said, smiling.

Ivory laughed out loud. "Lucian's ideas about how a career gets started are just slightly—idealized."

Lucian serenely ignored this. "Did Patty Bates like it?"

I told him exactly what happened, stopping now and then to explain the circumstances to Ivory. It was quite out of the question to condescend to him, or pity him. However unhappy he felt at heart—and I truly believed, and believe, he was unhappy—he was now thoroughly in control of the situation. He became expansive. He insisted on my sharing his wine with him; he teased Lucian; he drew me out. It was his party somehow—and it was a party. He produced some coke and we all did a few lines. Soon he managed to move close to me physically, took my hand, touched my arm on a pretext, gesturing, showing me how something happened. He took a mock swipe at Lucian, who answered in kind. He seemed to be having such a good time, to feel so much at home among these his dear friends, that it was impossible to uproot him. Hours went by. Despairing of ever talking to Lucian alone that night, I finally bowed out myself. I had to leave for Milk Lake at noon the next day; I needed to pack and get some sleep. We all went inside, they up to the living room so as not to disturb me. Mechanically I collected my clothes, filled the suitcase, undressed, went to bed. I didn't allow myself to think. The old chute opened before me. Just as I started the long slide down I heard the front door open and shut. Lucian appeared in my room.

"Are you sleeping?" he whispered.

"No, come in."

He sat down on the bed, his face at once proud and rueful. "Well. That's Ivory."

I thought about touching his hand, which lay unmoving

on the blankets. "Lucian, he loves you."

"I know," he answered, surprised.

"But he really loves you."

"I told you that. Don't you remember? I told you we both loved each other."

After a while I said, "Yes you did."

"He's really hurting. I don't know if you could see it—he's so phony. All that coke and laughing and fooling around . . ."

"That's not being phony, Lucian, that's just trying to save face. It's natural—especially in front of me. Anyway, I could see he was hurting, yes."

"He wants it to go on. But I told him it's over."

"You did?"

"Yes," he said, again in surprise, even in annoyance. "I told you all this. Don't you believe what I tell you?"

"Yes. I'm just—glad," I said.

"Why are you glad?"

"Because—" I paused, wondering if it was in Lucian to be coy. I didn't think so. "Because you know what you want. That's good."

"I guess so," he said dubiously. "I'd sure hate to be Ivory's age anyway and be as confused as he is." He yawned. "Anyway, I'm sorry about tonight Melanie—the show I mean."

"It's okay, don't worry about it." He started to bend down to kiss me good night but I stopped him. "Lucian, are you sure you're finished with Ivory?"

He gave a thin shriek of exasperation. "Would you try to help me, for God's sake? I mean, *please*. I'm trying to get *out* of the habit of caring about him, don't you see? It's just a habit; I can't listen to my feelings now because they're in the *habit* of caring about him. I have to listen to my—

my intellectual will, don't you understand? He doesn't know me. He doesn't listen to me. He just likes to—show me off—"

"Are you sure that isn't just because he does love you? You're so important to him."

"I don't care. It isn't *me* that's important to him, it's this *image* he has of me. I swear he doesn't listen to me. I told him all about you tonight and—you heard him, he thought you were a singer. He doesn't *listen*. He won't take me seriously. I told him about my monologue and all he could talk about was, I don't know, how much he thought it was like our situation or something. He has no understanding of art or talent or me or—anything. Okay? So I'm growing beyond it. Okay?"

"Okay."

"If you care about me, you'll help me."

"All right. All right."

He touched my face with his hand. "You see, you do listen to me—I think, anyway."

"I do."

"That's why I really love you." He kissed me. "You let me be honest. You let me be me."

I caught his hand in mine and kissed it. "Okay."

"So let's just don't talk about Ivory." He stood up.

"Right."

On the doorsill he stopped. "He is kind of interesting though, don't you think?"

His smile as he said this was full of the pleasure of ownership. I fumbled again for the sad chute. "Yeah, kind of," I muttered, turning over.

※

Lucian was still asleep when I left the next morning. I kissed him, set two alarm clocks so he wouldn't miss his appointment with Joan Dunbar, left a note and some cash where he could see it and quietly slipped from the house. I'd meant to call Patty before I left but the rush to the airport got the better of me. I figured I'd reach her on Monday. I was sorry to be returning to Milk Lane alone; even though Lucian would be coming the next day I didn't relish the prospect of reentering that circle unaccompanied by a fellow alien. Jules wasn't coming at all, which was a blessing when you considered that Lucian was, but on the other hand kind of disappointing. Jules has never been overly friendly to Donald since he and Megan moved in with Mother. Sibling-in-law rivalry, I guess. Personally I was glad to have someone keeping Mother occupied.

The plane to Boston was full of students returning to school that fall. It made La Guardia seem a little less tawdry and a little more like a large school bus stop. I felt awkward among the students, though all the time assuring myself that no one was paying attention to me. My life seemed so accidental and scrappy compared to theirs, which followed orderly seasons and schedules, all toward a recognizable goal. I knew this was only an illusion, that students' lives are perfect hotbeds of confusion, but it didn't make me feel at home among them. It was as if I'd crashed a party.

Unpleasant though it was I couldn't seem to stop thinking about Ivory. It was as if my meeting with him had left a raw, interesting place in my mind, a bruise I compulsively pressed and examined again and again. Image after image of him flashed through my tired head, sometimes that first poignant glimpse I'd had of his eyes, more often the painful, apparently laughing smile that replaced it. I had several phantom talks with him, there on the plane among the students. In one, noble and sad, we discussed our great mutual love for Lucian, and his for us; then, anguished but generous, sought a fair solution for all parties. In the next, I poured out a furious warning to him not to dare come near Lucian again, which was how Lucian wanted it (I said) and was damn well how it was going to be. There followed a short exegesis concerning Ivory's despicable selfishness in trying to open Lucian's wounds, and in the peroration a few succinct but forceful observations on my own creditable disinterestedness. Then I envisioned an accidental meeting among the three of us at La Guardia, as Lucian and I returned from the wedding. Lucian behaved very rudely indeed, and it was left to me to console poor Ivory. There were more scenes too. My encounter with him had shaken me. He was so different from what Lucian said; it made me wonder in what terms he spoke to Ivory about me.

At Logan I phoned home to make sure Lucian wasn't still sleeping. There was no answer, which was good. It was just time for him to be on his way to his interview. I tried Patty too but she was out of her office. It seemed useless to leave a message. Monday would do. I killed half an hour or so drinking grayish coffee and browsing among T-shirts celebrating Faneuil Hall and the like. By the time the tiny plane skittered down into Augusta I guessed the interview would have been finished. I fervently hoped it had gone well, because a step toward independence was, presumably, still a step away from Ivory. I wished Lucian could have flown up with me. I hadn't asked anyone to pick me up at Augusta, though Donald probably would have. The whole issue was too depressing to get involved with. I took the bus to Bruton, with the same driver as the last time (I didn't try to make jokes though) and at Bruton again climbed into Bobby Axelrod's cab. Bobby still didn't recognize me.

The day was dully warm, the trees still, the sky an indifferent white hanging low to the earth. The fact that summer was only a few days from its official conclusion seemed not to impress it much. Like the six a poker player blandly tosses while aces wait in his hand, this day seemed the casual discard of a season still sure of its strength. In fact, high summer never returned to Maine: there was a kind of diffuse heat through most of autumn, but the brash racket of mid-July had gone. I don't expect anyone to agree with me, Maine being so-called Vacationland and all, but in my opinion summer is no more native to Maine than the tourists who come and go with it. It's the wide white brush of winter, the Great Minimalist if you will, that reveals the state in its beautiful essence.

The point of my coming up Friday instead of the day of the wedding itself was to help take the edge off what I figured would be a tough evening at Milk Lake. Nothing I'd heard from my mother had made me believe she was any more reconciled to Donald's marriage than when I'd last seen her—though of course confidingness had not been at an all-time high between us since then. I'd told her Lucian was coming, for example, but I still hadn't said who he was; and she for her part had been pretty tight-lipped about politics at the farm. I trotted up to the door about four-thirty and found a wall-to-wall minefield. Megan, who let me in, was walking around like she had a gun with the safety off hidden inside her T-shirt. Rigid, sharp-eyed, humorless . . . No one was going to slip any tricks past her. Kissing her wasn't much fun; but being kissed by her was like a peek into the freezer. She kissed on assignment. Feed and clothe her, she kissed you. My mother authored the crime, and Sharon would never dream of forcing herself (as she would have conceived it) on Megan; but how had Donald permitted his daughter to drift alone so far to sea?

"Grandma's upstairs," said she, smiling the requisite smile for Aunt Melanie, "on the phone."

"Oh boy."

"Daddy and Sharon went shopping. They said Hi."

"Hi back. What are you doing?"

"Nothing."

"Come with me. I want to make some coffee." I led her through the ugly dining room into the kitchen, where Sharon had started a rib roast for dinner. The white sky through the window glazed the oak table with a cloudy half-shine. "Do you drink coffee yet?"

"Don't you think you'd better go up to Grandma?"

"She'll wait. Who's she talking to?"

"Mr. Flexner, I think."

"Oh Flexner, is it? That sounds inauspicious. Coffee?" She shook her head no. "Have you seen Benjy Dennison? Is he coming to the wedding?" I put water in the kettle and ruthlessly twirled the gas to high before striking a match. Megan's terrible self-control was making me want to be as noisy and reckless as possible. With a small scream I jumped back from the explosive blaze, tossing the match into the sink.

"Oh watch out!" squealed Megan, startled into spontaneity. I smiled, pleased.

"So. Benjy Dennison?"

"I don't know if he's coming. He's around somewhere I think."

"How are you doing?"

"Fine," she said at once. I had the feeling she'd decided this answer was safest long ago. Armour rule. Always say fine.

"Got that one right away," I said, raising an eyebrow. "Let's see how you do as the questions get tougher." She didn't smile back. She'd gotten control of herself again. I leaned on the counter sideways and watched her as she sat at the table. "Aren't you feeling kind of weird about having Donald marry again? I am."

No answer. Poor Megan. Like a large and stupid animal, I had crashed in one cloddish plunge through all the beautiful protocol she counted on to protect her. It was her only defense, and I was callously ignoring it. In this house you didn't ask questions. No matter how obvious tensions or hurts were you didn't notice them. Megan played the game. She'd agreed to follow the rules, perform her assigned part night and day. All she demanded in return was privacy: she and only she would know the truth of her interior condition. I was perfectly aware of what I was doing. I was breaching the terms of the treaty. Though it made me feel boorish and brutal I crashed on. It wasn't my treaty now.

"I mean, I like Sharon and all that," I said, "but it's going to be kind of strange to have her in the family, you know? And Amelia's going to be your sister, kind of. Pretty weird."

"I like them," she said faintly, hardly opening her mouth.

"So do I. Really." Could I in fact be poisoning her mind with ungenerous thoughts that had never come there before me? That's what my mother would have said, I was sure. Feeling vaguely bestial in a new way I nevertheless pushed on, "But don't you sort of feel like you're losing Donald too? I mean, maybe it's only me, but I've been thinking about Iris a lot."

I didn't want to say "your mother" and "your daddy." I didn't want her to feel I was talking to her as if to a child, condescendingly. I was only talking to her at all about this because I thought her feelings were so much what I would have felt. My mother had taught me that hostility was to emotion what sodomy was to sex: perversion. And open hostility was, by extension, an indecent display of perversion. I knew Megan had been indoctrinated with these interesting ideas, and it infuriated me to see her suffer shame as well as anger and fear. But I seemed to be getting nowhere. She watched me with the utmost suspicion and asked reluctantly, "What about her?"

I sat down and took her hand in mine. It lay there, stick-like and motionless. "How her life was . . . I was the flower girl when she got married. I went down the aisle just ahead of her and my father, and there Donald was, standing at the altar. I couldn't believe she was going to be a wife, like my mother. I thought it was the most amazing thing in the world. Nobody knew she was going to die so young."

Megan looked at me now with the mildest possible interest.

"So now that your father's getting married again," I went on, "I'm thinking a lot about her. Maybe Grandma is too. Aren't you?" Nothing. "I don't want to pry into your feelings, but if you did want to talk about—having a new mother . . ." I remembered that she'd been living with this prospect all the six weeks I had been in New York, if not longer. "I guess it's kind of late—"

"Sharon's not my mother," she broke in suddenly.

It was as honest as anything she'd ever told me. I was satisfied. "No, she's not," I agreed. "If you want to talk more any time, we can talk, okay? If not, not."

She removed her hand from mine and neatly laced it into her other one, placing her folded hands on the table just exactly in front of her. "Thank you. I don't care to talk."

"Okay."

"Okay." She returned to looking composedly indifferent. In the end my having broken the rules both disturbed and intrigued her I think: but most of all it alerted her to the fact that I was dangerous. For my own part, I felt clumsy, foolish, and obscurely mean. The teakettle whistled.

My mother was in a state of numbness, it appeared. She hardly looked at me when I sidled into her rosy nest; her official effusive politeness had never been less convincing. I was relieved. I'd been afraid of finding her melodramatic or hysterical, but she was quite matter-of-fact. I didn't believe for a minute she was resigned to the marriage, but I was purely grateful not to be forced to confront her unhappiness with her. If, as Megan had, she had buried her feelings, I had in her case no wish to unearth them. I slipped into her tone, answered politely and dishonestly her questions about Jules and "when my friend was coming" and, incredibly, avoided any talk of the wedding to take place so soon. We couldn't have skirted it more fastidiously if it had been some unspeakable sociopathic design. From her complexion and her thinness, it was clear to me that she was in bad health. She seemed light and papery, as if she'd been bleached in the sun and had all the color and damp of life baked out of her. I said nothing about it. I was tired of going around and around with her about doctors. She didn't like me to. It was her life. If she wanted to die, let her die. These were my thoughts. In retrospect, I believe the only words that passed between us that were the least bit to the point were: "I would have liked to see Jules again." I explained how busy he was and the subject was let drop. Don't get the idea that if Jules had come my mother would have paid any more attention to him than she did to me. She would not have. It was just the idea of his coming.

Donald and Sharon entered laughing; but even they had a strain of something electric and dangerous running between them. Donald hugged me. Sharon didn't. I liked her for not overdoing the imminent joy stuff. She was perfectly cordial. We gathered in the sitting room, just the three of us. Donald didn't look quite well either, though certainly better than on his return from Europe. They'd brought a Hello from Benjy, who was indeed in town and was coming to dinner. That cheered me. Sharon and Donald sat a little apart from each other on a salmon-pink Victorian love seat, one I used to read Frances Hodgson Burnett novels on when it rained in the summers. Their hands lay twined together between them on the stiffish brocade like two hairless animals curled up for warmth. The soft light of late afternoon soothed Sharon's sharp features and muffled the shadows on Donald's cheeks.

Talk among us had that uneasy searching quality that inevitably characterizes the first meetings of a pair of lovers with a friend. There was the feeling that we ought to find a style of conversation suitable for the three of us since, presumably, we would be meeting this way all the rest of our lives; but how much that communal style ought to partake of the one-to-one intimacies that fed it on each end was a tender and ticklish point. We nosed around tentatively here and there, all full of goodwill but afraid to intrude. After a time I asked where they would live.

"Your mother wants us to stay here," Donald told me, "or so she says."

"Oh yeah?"

"We're going to try it."

"You're kidding."

He laughed at my horrified look. "To tell you the truth, I don't like the idea of suddenly leaving her alone. Between the two evils—having us all here or having us all gone—I think the former is better. Don't you?"

"Better for whom?" I glanced at Sharon's blue eyes, neutral as a test pattern.

"I don't think she's well," Donald said.

"And . . . ?"

"I don't want to leave till I'm sure she's okay."

"You don't look too A-1 yourself."

He laughed again. "Nerves, that's all. I'm fine."

Sharon looked unimpressed. I don't think Dennisons set much store by nerves.

"Will you take a honeymoon?"

"A few days up at Bar Harbor, that's all."

"School starts for me soon," said Donald. "In fact, if you'll excuse me I want to look over the notes for my first lecture."

"I'll get back to my roast," said Sharon, not moving, as he kissed her good-bye.

"What will you do now?" I asked her.

She smiled. I felt a first glimmer of feeling from her, that warm, vaguely conspiratorial feeling that sometimes springs up between women when a man has just left them alone. "Mostly the same thing, I guess; only not paid. Amelia will take your room—at least, if you don't mind—"

I said of course not, which was the only acceptable answer. Unfortunately it was not true: I did mind. Armours are not good at moving over.

At dinner we observed all the technical forms of festivity. The Dennisons senior came, and with them Benjy. (Prescott Junior couldn't make the wedding, I discovered to my joy; when I can avoid being in the same room with two men I've slept with I always do.) Benjy behaved pretty much as if that night in New York had never happened. Not that he jumped all over me; but that wasn't his style anyway. He was just friendly and calm and open to whatever. Mrs. Dennison, vigorous and plain, sat and suffered to be waited upon. I think she was happy Sharon was finally to be made an honest woman. My pale mother was glacially courteous to everyone. Megan sat between her father and Amelia, remote as a lunar landscape. Generally speaking I think we all drank as much wine as we possibly could. Between the first course and the entree Benjy and I sneaked out and smoked a joint. Donald toasted his new mother-in-law, his fiancée, and my mother. Sharon and I served, which gave us an excuse to get out of the room now and then. Mr. Dennison's tie, like a thin, evil serpent, seemed to threaten to strangle his long neck. He referred repeatedly to Amelia and Megan as "the girls," which made Megan visibly wince. Amelia got overexcited and spilled her ice water onto Megan's plate. Benjy rubbed his long leg up against mine under the table. I toasted the bride and groom. It was a dismal affair.

Afterward Sharon went home with her folks. Benjy and I cleaned up; then he left in Sharon's car. Donald had followed the Dennisons home to be with Sharon a little longer. Megan and I played Scrabble after the dishes were done. My mother sat with us, reading, till Donald got back, then counterfeited a yawn and went upstairs just before he got into the house. I left Megan (who was seventy points ahead of me anyway) alone with her father, hoping against hope she'd open up to him. Then I was free to call Lucian at last; I was very curious to know how the interview with Joan Dunbar had gone.

The phone rang six or seven times before he picked up.

"Oh, Melanie—I was just leaving," he said.

"How'd it go?"

"How'd what go? Oh, the interview; great. I'm sorry, I'm just so scattered this minute—"

"Why? What's up?"

"Oh nothing, just— The interview went great, really fine. I liked her. I think she liked me."

"Well that's good."

"But listen, Melanie, can I get back to you later or something? I'm just—" He gave an expressively vocalized sigh and left the sentence unfinished.

"Yes, sure." I felt awkward and strangely chastened. Calling someone at an inopportune moment has always filled me with guilt. "Where are you going so fast?"

"Oh nowhere. I mean—Ivory asked me if I'd have dinner over there. He still wants to talk. I don't know, I guess I feel like I should. Do you think I should?"

"You should if you want to. What happend to Gary?"

"I think they broke up," he said. "God Melanie, you're one of the most important people on earth to me, you know?"

"I'm glad."

"You are, really. I just love you. I'm really grateful to you for setting that interview up. I mean, not that that's why I love you—"

"I get it."

"You're just really special to me. I think you understand me better than anyone else, you know? Not everyone finds people to understand them, I think. It's really rare and really important."

"I'm glad you feel that way," I said.

"I better run now. I'll see you tomorrow."

I reminded him his flight left at eight-thirty.

"Oh damn, that's right. I'm going to have to get up, what, at seven tomorrow?"

"At least."

"Oh, damn. Because I'm going to be up late tonight, I think—"

There was a long pause. "So what do you want to do?" I asked finally.

"Let me see if I can arrange for a little later flight, okay? I'll call you. The wedding's not till two-thirty, right?"

"Right; but Lucian, if I'm going to pick you up—"

"I know, I have to get in earlier. Just let me check around—I'll have Ivory's driver look into it maybe; he's good at this stuff."

"Why don't you just take the flight I—"

"Don't worry about it. If it doesn't work out I'll just get up early. Don't worry. I'll call you either way tomorrow morning and let you know when I get in. All right?"

I agreed.

The evening at Milk Lake had fallen apart completely as far as festivity went. My mother was already in bed; I found Donald at his desk reading Keats and Megan's door shut. Admitting defeat, I crawled up to the slope-roofed room that contained the piano. The air had grown chilly. Sometime around midnight I even saw a few lost, confused flakes of snow. They melted as they approached the lingering warmth of the house.

Lucian's birthday was coming up. I was writing a song to give to him. I worked on it till late that night, stopping every forty-five seconds or so to think about where he was. I wondered if while he was up in Maine I might be able to tell him what I'd meant to say the previous evening. I was still replaying those scenes with Ivory too, real and imagined. As for my showcase, it seemed as if it had taken place ages ago. Patty had said she loved my performance but that wasn't the same as saying it was good; and she hadn't mentioned the songs at all. I had a feeling Helicon and I were not going to see things eye to eye. I didn't look forward to Monday.

When I went downstairs to bed the house was in darkness, not even a hall light left on for me. No one had come up to say good-night either. It gave me a real crummy feeling.

In the morning there were difficulties. Sharon wasn't there to cook breakfast and no one could find what she'd done with the spatula. One of the heels on Megan's pumps dropped off, apparently without provocation. Donald picked up a cast-iron pan and seared his right hand. Mother broke a nail. Lucian didn't call me.

I don't think my mother had slept much, if at all. About noon she called down the steep wooden steps for me to come help her fasten the soft gray dress she had bought for the wedding. I found her fully made up and stockinged, mincing around gingerly to find her balance in a new pair of very high-heeled shoes. The thin spiky heels melted into the thick pile of the red carpet while the unscraped soles slithered and glided capriciously. My mother wore the least comfortable shoes of any woman I know. She had a genius for finding them. After a turn or two here and there she tottered over to me, presenting me with her back. "Where's your friend?" she asked.

I said "I don't know," silently cursing the fussy little

hooks at the neck of her dress. "He was supposed to call." I hadn't been this close to my mother in years, except for brief kisses. She let me touch her so rarely. The unnatural odor of Arpège rose from her freshly soaped skin. This simple act of buttoning her dress woke in my hands and neck a long chain of flip-flopping associations: her fingers buttoning my buttons, fluttering along my spine, mine along hers, hers along mine. There's something so pleasurable and intimate, albeit incidental, in the gentle drumming flurry of a woman's fingers on the nape of one's neck. In me it evokes a warm dreamy state like a trance. Having a woman wash my hair does the same thing. Watching my own hands fumble before me hypnotized me similarly, only with an added shade of tender, if somewhat officious, love for her.

"Maybe he isn't coming."

"Drop your head forward." There was a hook with a rope-let of threads instead of an eye that was being especially recalcitrant. My mother pitched slightly forward and back on her wicked heels as the weight of her lowered head unbalanced her. "I don't know. He tends to be late a lot."

"If he's very much later, you won't have time to pick him up, Melanie."

"Yes, I know. That's just the problem." I patted her collar. "There."

"Now where are my pearls? Melanie, what are you going to wear?"

"Oh, I have a dress," I mumbled, unpleasantly aware that what I had brought she would not consider appropriate. I hadn't owned a dress my mother would consider appropriate for a wedding in years and years.

"Did you bring gloves?"

"Gloves?" I repeated blankly.

"Yes. Did you forget them? I can lend you some."

"It's not the kind of dress you wear gloves with," I said.

"What kind of dress is that? Let me see it—"

"No, don't bother. Is that the phone?"

"No."

"I thought I heard it ring in the kitchen."

"When the phone rings, it rings in here too," my mother said. "Melanie, I hope you've brought something appropriate to wear."

"I'll go get dressed."

"I can lend you something—"

"No thank you. I know what I have will be fine. Have you noticed the rain, Mother?" I went on quickly. "It looks as if it means to keep up all day."

"Your friend isn't going to make it," she said, with a glance at the clock on her nightstand.

"Yes. Never mind that." The spell of intimacy had been thoroughly broken by now. I was unable to keep my annoyance out of my voice. "I'll go get ready."

"All right. Do you have an umbrella, dear?"

"I have a raincoat and rain hat."

"A rain hat, dear? Won't that ruin your hairstyle?"

"For God's sake Mother, does my hair look as if it had a style? I forgot there was such a thing."

"I only asked—"

"I know. Thank you. I appreciate your concern. I am fine. I have everything. I'm going now and get dressed."

"All right. Will you help Megan, please?" she called to me as I left the room.

"Okay."

"Don't let her comb her hair on her own. She really doesn't know how to do it."

"I won't. Don't worry. For Christ's sake."

I don't think she heard the last words. I was pretty much out of the door.

Lucian still hadn't called. I'd brought a two-piece, mauvish, designer-sweatshirty outfit, with a very short, divided skirt. I wore boots, hoping my mother would not have a chance to notice my unstockinged knees. Megan seemed to have done her hair fine; in fact, she required no help now that Donald had nailed the heel back on her shoe. She rather resented my presence, it seemed, than otherwise. Ready myself, I retreated as ever to the piano; half an hour later Megan called up the stairs that it was time to be going. I stepped into my bedroom to get my raincoat. From the landing outside my mother's door I saw Donald and Megan waiting by the newel post. Sharon had waxed all the floors in the house that week (preparing her own new home to receive her) and the old wooden steps were especially treacherous. I clung to the railing as I came down. Donald, distracted, smiled at me absently. Megan declined even to meet my eyes. As I joined them she was looking beyond me, up toward my mother's door.

Mother was just coming out. On the landing she paused a minute, her eyes meeting Megan's, then mine (I thought I saw in them disapproval of my outfit), then Donald's. She smiled a little wearily. Then she stepped out, lost her footing, wobbled, slipped, toppled, smashed to the ground and, rolling over and over, racketed all the way down the slick narrow staircase. She slid to a stop on the last steps, just an inch or two from my booted feet.

FIFTEEN

≫⊱

MY MOTHER LAY with her head bottommost, her face to the floor and sort of wedged down into the angle between the first and second steps. From her shoulders up, however, she was lying on her back. Her feet, which should have been sprawled across the staircase, were crossed at the ankles and perched, neat in their new gray shoes, somewhere about the seventh step up. Donald, who was standing by me, wanted to move her. I wouldn't let him. I knew, sort of as an interesting fact, that you don't touch people who have fallen like that. I sent him and Megan into the kitchen to phone for an ambulance and hide.

My mother was so delicately balanced where she lay that I feared every moment some slowly accumulating force of gravity would topple her over again, making her perform one last somersault. I kept worrying about the awkwardness of her position, the grotesqueness of it. You could see her right leg up to the thigh. I was unwilling to think of my mother as an injured person, as a person who has had a terrible fall. For the sake of decorum if nothing else I mentally reversed her descent and made her fall up the staircase. I did this again. It comforted me.

Donald came in to tell me the ambulance was on its way. I thanked him. "Why don't you stay with Megan?" I said.

"You might as well keep her out of here."

He drifted vaguely back into the kitchen.

Secretly I knew my mother was dead. But I didn't want to say it yet. I didn't even want to know it. I wanted to be on my way to Donald's wedding; I wanted things to be as they were before. For a few minutes the two states, the two ideas, held equal sway in my mind. Then, slowly, the new truth supplanted the old one. My mother wasn't breathing. Nothing about her moved. She was dead.

I was glad I could not see her face. For a while her broken body struck me as having a strange kind of innocence, a sweetness, about it. Deprived of personality, of personal history, it was like a child's body, like Eve's before she took the apple. Even so, I was increasingly aware of a kind of zone forming all around her, electric with warning: death, it was. Sickening. After an interval of some twenty minutes, during which I threw up twice, the ambulance arrived.

I let the paramedics in. They rushed at once to my mother; but when they got there I realized with an inner quiver that they were not going to touch her either. They asked if they could use the phone. I waved them toward the kitchen and went to the sitting room to wait. Donald and Megan came out. We didn't say anything to each other. Within half an hour the house was full of people. The paramedics called the state police; the state police called the State Investigator. My mother had had what they called an accidental death, and everyone seemed to want to know about it. Somebody even phoned a reporter from the *Bruton Bee*, or maybe she picked it up from the police band on the radio. She made us all coffee.

Once the State Investigator had taken pictures of my mother her body could be moved. They put her on a stretcher and carried her into the living room, where the medical technician from the ambulance—Steve, his name was—poked and tested her. Meantime the State Investigator asked Donald and Megan and me questions calculated to find out which of us had pushed her off the landing. It was a nightmare, like being in a huge set of Clue suddenly come to life.

The medical technician came in and announced that my mother had broken her neck. Since this did not qualify as a previously existing medical condition, he explained, an autopsy would have to be performed to determine the cause of death. I didn't want an autopsy performed on my mother; besides, it seemed to me that if her neck was broken that was cause of death enough; but I made only a half-hearted attempt at arguing the point, and then I gave up. With all these people in the house my mother seemed to be everyone's business but ours. I was relieved when they all went away.

Of course, by now the Dennisons were curious to know where we were. Mr. Dennison had phoned twice but had hung up none the wiser for having spoken to Donald, whom the events of the day were increasingly depriving of the ability to frame a simple English sentence. By the time the State Investigator left, in fact, I think Donald had been on the point of confessing to doing the deed himself, in the Conservatory, with the Lead Pipe. Mr. Dennison gave up calling and sent Benjy over in person to ask. It wasn't until I saw Benjy, I think, that I really started to understand what had happened.

Megan let him in. We were now on Megan's emotional turf—a world where people, especially mothers, do tend to drop dead without notice—and, superficially at least, she was the least rattled of the three of us. From the dining room I heard her open the door to Benjy and politely ask if she could take his wet coat and his umbrella. Then she said very composedly, "If you don't mind waiting here a minute I'll get Melanie for you." Which she did.

I walked into Benjy's arms and stood there a full minute or two. Then he looked down at me and I moved back a little from him and told him, "My mother's dead." Involuntarily, I turned away as the words came out. My face crumpled. I felt ashamed of what I was saying, as of an intimate and indecent confession. I started to cry. He pulled me closer so I could cry against him but I found that with the thing said I didn't want to be near him. I backed away. "If you would just tell Sharon and everyone," I mumbled. "It was an accident. She fell down the stairs." I got this out fairly clearly; but inside me swelled and breathed a mass of rage, outrage, that I had to swallow constantly to keep down. It expanded every second, like the shapeless creature in a science fiction film.

"Can I do anything?"

"No, she's gone. To the hospital; they took her away." I reached out purposelessly and touched the damp edge of his white cuff. It was odd to see Benjy in a coat and tie. "Donald might want to see Sharon, if you could send her over."

I loved him for not hanging around and making things worse. Anyone else might have stayed, made phone calls, asked questions, insisted. Benjy just left, and that was the right thing. I wanted to be alone.

First though I realized I ought to call Jules. I went into the empty kitchen. Informing him of what had happened across the double barrier of my pain and his unpreparedness was like pulling him through two hoops of fire. It seemed impossibly cruel. To manage it I sort of unhinged my feelings from my mind. Dispassionately and with great clarity, I told him this awful story about his mother. I felt so sorry for him. At the same time I wondered sporadically if my mother oughtn't to be showing up soon.

He said he'd fly up at once.

"Somebody should call Norman Flexner. You want me to?"

"I'll do it."

"Jules—"

I couldn't think how to finish this sentence. We both hung up the phone. This done, I was free to go upstairs and be by myself for a while if I wanted. I wasn't sure where Donald and Megan were but I assumed they were together and looking after each other. I didn't go up just then though. Instead I dialed my apartment in New York. I still hadn't heard from Lucian. I told myself I was calling him; but really I think I was calling myself—the self I'd detached in order to speak to Jules. Anyway nobody answered.

When I went upstairs I realized what I'd been avoiding. But there was no stain on the staircase to show where my mother had fallen. There was no mark of any kind, not even a strayed glove. The only disorder she'd left behind I saw as I passed the door of her bedroom, still ajar as she'd left it: her large everyday purse, open on the bed and ransacked of the necessaries she'd transferred to her small new dove-gray clutch. The clutch, improbably, had gone with her to the hospital.

I went to my bedroom—which should have been Amelia's by now—and sat in the window seat. I think when somebody dies bits of the people who loved them must also be surrendered in so many smaller deaths. Now it felt as if my sympathetic death would kill me too. The sudden eradication of my mother from this earth had none of the aching tenderness that had tinged the idea of losing her. On the contrary, it was heavy and cold as an ax. The power of death made me sick to my stomach, as would the mean, petty power of a contemptible bully. There was no awesome magnificence to it, nor were my feelings melancholy or bittersweet. I had learned this all before, when Iris died; and before that when my father died: but some sensations are so nearly unbearable you forget them the moment you can. In this case it was the fact of my mother's never having needed my love that was most painful.

After a while, I got the idea that maybe I should check on Megan. I looked all over upstairs without finding her, then glanced into the kitchen and dining room. Nothing. In the sitting room I found Donald. He looked preoccupied but not very upset. "Where's Megan?" I asked.

He shrugged.

"Are you okay?"

He didn't answer. I was put off. I wasn't exactly tops myself.

I turned to go. "If you see Megan, tell her I'm looking for her."

"Oh Melanie, do we have any salve or ointment or something for my hand? I burnt it."

"I know."

"I shouldn't have touched that pan with my bare hand."

"I don't live here Donald, you do. Why don't you check the medicine chest?"

But he didn't move. I left, still irritated. I finally realized Megan had gone outside, notwithstanding the weather, to visit her rock by the lake. I went out myself and got close enough to make sure she was there, but I left her her privacy. On the way back I thought mean thoughts about Donald, and what little care he seemed to take of his daughter. The lake and the sky were the same whitey-gray color. A few feet off from the shoreline you couldn't tell where the mist off the water ended and the low drifts of cloud began. The rain had diminished to a drizzle. At the kitchen door I found Sharon, on her way in through the back by force of habit I suppose. We told each other how sorry we were. I sent her along to Donald.

She was back in the kitchen before I got upstairs. "Did Donald ask for me to come here?"

"What?"

"Donald doesn't want me in the house. That's what he just said."

"You're kidding."

"No; he says he should never have touched me." She dropped back against the refrigerator door. She wore a peach-colored dress with a square collar edged with peachy lace and an A-line skirt a little on the short side. Pinned to her bodice was a bunch of tiny, peachy roses. If they had a fragrance I couldn't smell it.

I found I was not terribly interested in her plight. "Whatever you think you should do—" I began, gesturing largely toward the house and Donald; but Megan came in and I broke off. Her eyes were pink. The wind slammed the door shut behind her.

"Hello," she whispered, and went on through the kitchen.

"Where are you going?" I asked.

She paused without turning. Rain trembled in her hair. "My room."

"Oh. Can I dry you off?"

"I'll do it." She went out and through the dining room. We heard her light steps, slow in her unaccustomed pumps, start up the stairs.

"I don't like that," I said. I was still dressed in my chic sweatshirt and the very short culottes that went with it. Ridiculous, as usual. "I think I'll go after her."

Sharon nodded. She must have left soon after. I didn't see her again till the funeral.

"Megan? Can I come in?" I held my ear next to her closed door as if this could help me get nearer her.

"No please. I'm okay, I mean." In a thin, high voice.

"For a minute?" I opened the door anyway, which was ratty of me, and leaned in.

"I'm okay," she repeated. She was carefully untwisting the rubber bands from her wet and disordered pigtails, sitting at a little painted vanity table my mother had bought for Iris. She didn't turn to face me but we could see each other reflected in the mirror. The message in her eyes was clear.

"All right. I'm up top with the piano if you want me," I said. "Don't be afraid to come up."

"Okay," said Megan, watching in the mirror till I'd shut her door.

I went upstairs. The piano reminded me of Lucian—his birthday song was on the music rack—and after a while I went back down to send a telegram to the apartment. It said, "My mother has died in an accident. Please call me." I got Martin Ivory's address from information and sent one there too, since that's where Lucian had been going. I found that every time I told the news again I felt different about it. I'd told it four times now: Benjy, Jules, and the two telegrams. If it could be told in a dozen words, four times in four hours, how awful could it be? But every time was painful. A new kind of time was going by: hours that I was alive and my mother was not. Sometimes it felt like my heartbeat was a ticking. Repeating aloud that my mother was dead intensified the tick.

Jules hadn't wanted me to pick him up at the airport but of course I did. He came in at ten o'clock. About eight I'd made supper for Donald and Megan and me, the same thing we'd had for breakfast, plus leftovers from the previous night. Food tastes peculiar in the wake of a crisis, if you taste it at all. A meal takes on its own shape, like a work of art, and you don't forget it. We had scrambled eggs and cold roasted potatoes and orange juice and sad broccoli. There was roast beef left too but no one could face meat. Donald seemed more concerned with his burnt hand than anything else. He was bringing a whole new meaning to the words sitting room. That's where he'd been when I announced supper and that's where he went as soon as he'd finished. He'd been there all day, sitting. At the table he looked moony and ate with his left hand. Megan continued inscrutable.

I can think of about six thousand nights I liked better than that one. I don't imagine anyone actually slept more than an hour or two. Jules didn't want to use my mother's bed, so I gave him mine, and I moved into Megan's room. She had white-covered twin beds, side by side, like two big loaves of sugar. I was relieved by Jules's arrival. I wanted someone to help me, and Donald was no use at all. For the first time in my life it was important that I act like a grownup: keep order, decide things, look strong. Megan could not be left to get her own food and puzzle this death out alone;

and neither could Donald, who was functioning considerably less smoothly than she. Jules at least was able. All Armours are able.

Jules and I didn't mention our feelings at all to each other, even when we were alone; we only talked about how it had happened and what was to be done now. But he helped. He called the hospital and arranged to have a funeral home pick up our mother. He gave them permission to embalm her. In the morning, he and I went there together. Reluctantly, I left Megan with Donald, who was now more obsessed with his hand than ever, though it was not a bad burn. He refused to use it at all. He even asked Megan to tie his shoes. By then I had no patience with him whatever; it seemed my affection for him had been utterly eroded by twenty-four hours of simple annoyance.

The reception room of the Arrow-Demarest Funeral Home swarms with the kind of furniture you win on television, fabulous Broyhill or something. Crocheted doilies decorate heavily upholstered chairs; hardbound books, mostly high school text books, jam corner cupboards. Our counselor, so-called, was Wayne Demarest, a pale-haired, purple-cheeked man, a middle-aged hustler with a sharp eye out for the main chance. He beckoned us into his office and gave us cups of coffee we didn't want. His office was lined with flocked wallpaper, deep red, like the inside of a strep throat. It was at the center of the building and so without windows. The whole building was full of tiny windowless rooms, like a sinister hotel. Jules sat very far forward on his vinyl chair, as if to leave room for the invisible person who really occupied it. I tucked my hands under my thighs and watched Mr. Demarest mistrustfully. My coffee cooled on the arm of my chair; it was instant, mixed with Cremora, and was fast acquiring a kind of patina.

We did the paperwork for the death certificate first. Mr. Demarest insisted on referring to my mother as the Beloved or the Departed and to Jules and me as the Bereaved. As he recorded her name and birthplace and so on he ran his left index finger along the black lines. Mr. Demarest had beautiful hands. His pink nails were rimmed with a fluting of white at the tip like the curling edge of a tiny petal.

You're supposed to know where your parents' parents were born, which neither Jules nor I did. We had an embarrassing number of "unknowns" left on the form by the time we were done. We discussed life insurance, then flowers, music, obituaries, death notices—we had one sent to the local paper in Sands Point to alert her old friends there—pallbearers, eulogies, what she should be buried in . . . I mean clothes. Mr. Demarest asked the religion of the deceased. Jules and I looked guiltily at one another. "No religion," said Jules.

"If you desire a nondenominational ceremony," he offered, "I can officiate myself."

"That will be fine," I said tightly.

Mr. Demarest smiled. "Very well, then. Now the next thing . . . If you'll just follow me—" He rose. We did too. Mr. Demarest then led us down twisting, insubstantially wainscotted corridors to a large high-ceilinged showroom. We stepped inside and found ourselves waist-deep in coffins, twenty or thirty of them, gaping, each glutted with lace. Each just man-length, with a tiny pillow like a baby's, a narrow parody of a bed. "Any of them," I gasped, going out. A price card nestled in the lace inside each casket. Mr. Demarest was already explaining to Jules the value of gasket sealers as I left.

I leaned against the wall of the corridor, weak-kneed, waiting for Jules. My mother's body was nearby somewhere, probably in a freezer in a plastic bag. I didn't want to think of it. I concentrated instead on her spirit, if such a thing there was or is, and wondered where it might have gone. To my father? To Iris? A couple in sneakers and shorts drifted past me, their voices hushed, eyes downcast. I had the idea Iris was getting a big kick out of all this mess. After all, she was dead; you couldn't expect her to be horrified. She had that kind of sense of humor too—a little on the cosmic side. Here Donald had at last been about to win a match with Mother and what happened? Mother sacrifices her queen but leaves Donald permanently in checkmate. And ends the tournament.

Jules was out in a very few minutes, having picked I never asked what kind of casket. There was another thing in that room too, a pink filmy dress with a satin underslip, very narrow, hanging near a mahogany coffin and marked $49. You could buy it if you had to bury a woman who'd been ill so long that she didn't own any day clothes. I don't know how Jules managed to stay in there long enough to choose whatever it was he did choose. He emerged looking sub-aquatic.

"Let's go home," I said.

"But the burial vault, Miss Armour—"

"Mr. Demarest says we need a burial vault."

I stood still and turned to face him in the middle of the hallway. "What is a burial vault?"

Mr. Demarest explained that even with a good casket such as the one we picked, a burial vault was necessary to ensure protection.

"Protection from what?"

"From the elements."

"The elements. I see. And what exactly," I asked, "are we protecting from the elements?"

"The beloved," said Mr. Demarest simply; but he looked embarrassed at having been pushed to say so much.

"The beloved in question," I said, "is dead."

"Melanie, let's go home."

"If there's any time, for example, you don't need to worry about protection, I think we can safely say it would be when a person is dead. I think we can safely venture that when a person has died—"

Jules was firm in cutting me off. Seeing the chance to take control he overcame his nausea and marched me out of the mortuary. Later he phoned Mr. Demarest, who had hurriedly slipped him a pamphlet from a burial vault manufacturer as we went. I think we ordered the SR/Trilene model. It has a stainless steel inner lining and an extra-heavy concrete lid.

The funeral took place Monday. Hardly anyone came who could get out of it. My father's brother, whom we had called, sent a telegram from Arizona. My mother didn't have any family anymore. Norman Flexner flew up Sunday night, so he was there, and the Dennisons came of course, and a few other locals—Mother's doctor, the Bruton librarian, the Feiwels, whom I remembered vaguely from my childhood summers, three or four couples I didn't know— and naturally, Donald and Megan and Jules and me. And Donald's burnt hand, I should add, which was now assuming a character all its own. Donald treated it as if it were something he owned or knew and (reluctantly) was responsible for, but not as a part of himself. He carried it by its wrist, dangling from his left hand like a small tattered purse. Dr. Corbin, noticing this, offered to take a look and treat it but Donald wouldn't let him near. He wouldn't let Sharon get near him either. His attitude toward her took its flavor roughly from the nunnery scene in *Hamlet*. I truly believe English professors should be debriefed every five years to get the high tragedy out of their heads. If this procedure had been followed with Donald, it would probably have saved us endless trouble.

There had been no question as to where the burial would take place, since before my father died he bought a double plot in Stone Ridge, a nondenominational cemetery outside Webster. His monument there read

ARMOUR
Husband
Abraham Gerald
1912–1972
Wife
Beatrice Schaefer
1914–19

So all we had to do was have 81 chiseled in and the grave was complete.

What ceremony there was took place at the graveside. Down east they say, "If you don't like the weather, wait a minute." When we got to Stone Ridge the sun was high and hot; Saturday's rain had vanished and the maintenance men had clearly been out watering the grass. We gathered for convenience' sake at the door to the mausoleum, a tall building in which shiny gray marble banks of vaults could be seen rising in austere and elegant monotony from floor to ceiling. Bunches of red flowers bristled out at nearly every door, as if sprung from the stone. At the very top of the building, two large windows stood open to admit the breeze.

At a little after one o'clock Mr. Demarest gave me the go-ahead and Jules and I led our party to the grave. The air was soft; a pleasant wind swept past us. We walked over damp, new-cut grass which should have smelled sweet but instead seemed to give off a tainted and unwholesome odor, a smell that lingered in my nostrils for weeks. We walked carefully around a new grave with fresh clods of earth and grass scattered around its margins. Bits of damp cut grass stuck in clumps to the smaller monuments that studded the rolling ground. I glanced at one:

BABY

John Erskine

June 8, 1923

it read. Just that. There was a whole row of BABY monuments like that, with only one date, in fact rows and rows. A flock of birds suddenly took off from among them, squawking. At my side Jules's silent profile sliced the air, wearing a surprised and bewildered expression. From a corner of the cemetery, behind a parking lot, tapping noises rose from the Webster Monument Company into the afternoon. Jules awkwardly touched my shoulder.

"Are you okay?"

I nodded.

I was glad to reach my father's grave and to read his familiar name. I hadn't been here since his funeral. We found Mother's side had been dug already but the hole was covered with planks and Jell-O green astroturf. Her coffin stood alongside it, closed. It gave me a horrible feeling to think of her face looking up at that lid. And now we were going to drop the whole box into a second box in a hole and cover it up with dirt. An image of her alive and frantically struggling to get out of the boxes flashed through my mind sporadically for days.

The mourners gathered around the grave. I asked Megan to stand by me and held her limp hand in mine. Jules cried. I cried. Norman Flexner talked about how special my mother was, how my father had loved her, and how he had come to know both of them. I never liked Norman Flexner. The next plot over belonged to Howard and Mayanne Chase, d. 1953 and 1955 respectively. Despite the remoteness of those years a jar of white daisies had been left on their graves. The jar had been knocked over and the flowers had dried almost beyond recognition. Norman Flexner stopped talking. Mr. Demarest asked if anyone else would care to speak. Benjy Dennison, who stood almost directly across from me (with Sharon half-hidden behind him), caught my eye and looked questioningly at me. I shook my head. I had nothing to say, or else too much. Jules coughed and choked on some tears. He blew his nose in a large linen handkerchief he must have had since grade school. The sky, which had been almost empty ten minutes before, began to fill with clouds. An energetic burst of wind brushed through us, lasting longer than we expected and startling me, at least. Mr. Demarest looked to Donald, who had said he might like to speak. Donald glanced down at his injured hand, opened his mouth as if to say something and shut it again. His eyes, bleared from sleeplessness, rested on the coffin a moment, then turned dully up to Sharon and stayed there. And that was that. Mr. Demarest thanked the mourners for coming and everyone shook themselves and realized it was over. I keep forgetting to mention I hadn't heard from Lucian at all.

We didn't stay to see the casket lowered. Everyone drifted back toward the mausoleum, shook hands and departed. The sky was thick with clouds by now, the air charged with a heavy dampness. Megan had to go to the bathroom before we left and so did I. We went together. In the bathroom, as we were washing our hands, I caught her reflection in the mirror. Her eyes were pink with repressed tears, but she looked to me as if she were laughing, or rather, trying not to. For a moment I was shocked; then, to my astonishment, I heard myself snort, then giggle. Immediately, Megan erupted too. It was over as soon as it began, just those two little bursts of hysteria. I bent over and washed my face with very cold water, and gulped it down too. Megan followed my example. Then we dried ourselves briskly and severely with harsh paper towels. I wanted to tell her it was all right, that it was only the tension; but I think she knew. When we left the bathroom, cheeks bright from the rough towels, I'm sure everyone thought we'd been crying together.

We drove home through a thin rain under a seagull-colored sky. I almost fell asleep to the steady click-sweep-click of the windshield wipers. Norman Flexner being in something of a hurry to get back to New York asked if he could read Mother's will to us when we got back to the house. We ate something first, in the kitchen. Within half an hour the rain had stopped; the sky darkened to the color of pewter. Megan, still in her funeral dress, went out to walk by the lake. The rest of us—Donald, Jules, Norman and me—filed into the dining room, I don't know why, because it was so ugly I guess.

Norman sat at the head of the table, where my mother used to sit. He is a compact man of middle height and middle age. One imagines him playing squash at the Athletic Club. He is a connoisseur of wines, a womanizer of some distinction, a fastidious and unhappy man. From his slender attaché case he drew a set of papers and a pair of bifocals. The thick lenses split the dark twin worlds of his eyes in half. From these divided depths he watched us attentively.

Jules sat across from him, in my father's place. His eyes were clear again and only his red-rimmed nostrils showed he'd been crying. He kept jumping around in his chair, pushing at the arms as if to get rid of them—only the two end chairs of that set have arms, and I think he wasn't used to them. Donald and I sat opposite each other in armless children's chairs, Donald on what used to be Jules's and my side, I in Iris's old place. Donald was still holding his hand as if it were something faintly disgraceful; during the funeral he'd begun to let it droop lower, almost in front of his crotch, as if to cover it. At the table though he set it before him, laying it down gently, joint by joint, like a tiny white sleeping cat. He paid close attention to it. About midway through the reading his eyes began to stream with tears, apropos of nothing in particular it seemed. He hadn't been shaving, not even for the funeral, and his two stripes of beard showed as blue shadows in the sunless afternoon.

"'Be it remembered that I, Beatrice Schaefer Armour of Webster, County of Kennebec and State of Maine, being of lawful age and of sound and disposing mind and memory, but mindful of the uncertainty of life, do make, publish and declare this my last will and testament, hereby revoking all former wills by me made.'" So Norman Flexner began. The will was dated August 14, 1981. I realized later she must have been writing to change it that day I stormed out of Milk Lake. Her previous will had been made in 1974. There was a great deal of legal folderol concerning the administration of the estate, the more so as considerable property was at stake, but Norman rattled through it at a good clip, knowing no one was really listening anyway. I myself was reflecting on the soundness of my mother's memory, taken as a literal and not a legal concept. When he reached the bequests Norman's voice changed unmistakably. He fixed each of us with his bisected eyes before revealing what was ours, and cleared his throat between clauses.

The substance of the new will was this: to Jules went intact the controlling interest in my father's paper company, which my mother had maintained all these years, with provisions that he was to keep for himself fifty percent of the income derived from the holdings. Twenty-five percent of the income went to me, for the purpose of maintaining myself and also Milk Lake, which was now mine. The other twenty-five percent was to be used for Megan at Jules's discretion, the remainder of this part, if any, to be held in trust for her till she was twenty-one. Jules also received miscellaneous stocks and bonds, to do with what he liked. A thousand dollars was left to our old housekeeper in Sands Point, if she was still alive. Some land in northern Maine went to Megan. Mother's personal effects were left to me, to keep or sell, except a few named pieces of jewelry left to Megan, and her engagement ring, which went to Jules.

Donald wasn't mentioned.

After the reading Norman Flexner took a cab to the airport. Megan came in from outdoors and I told her, because I thought someone should, what was hers. Jules stayed the night at the Lake but Tuesday morning he left too. He insisted on taking a taxi. In the driveway I kissed him goodbye, more or less, then reentered the house alone. My mother was buried, her business settled. This house was mine. Somewhere inside it sat Iris's husband and her child. My parents were dead.

SIXTEEN

꙰

TUESDAY AFTERNOON, the day after the funeral, the phone rang.

"Oh. Lucian."

"Hi."

I couldn't think what to say and neither could he. I was standing by the window in the empty kitchen. I started to hang up the phone.

"I didn't know about your mother till just now," he said. I heard him even though the receiver was no longer at my ear.

"What?" I listened again.

"I didn't get your telegram till today." There was another silence. The connection was clear enough when we talked, but when we were quiet I could hear half of a conversation between two women in New York whose wires were somehow mixed up with ours. The voice I could hear was intelligible though faint. *She couldn't pick them both up while she was at it?* It paused and resumed, *So he takes the bus home; it won't kill him.*

"Melanie?" Lucian said. "I'm sorry."

I said nothing.

. . . too sensitive. That's—

"I guess there's no right thing to say now," Lucian went on. His voice sounded so sweet to me, like music, like honey.

Honey, people take advantage.

"I was out in Southampton with Ivory all weekend. Oh God, Melanie, I didn't know. I tried to call you on Saturday to tell you I wasn't coming but nobody answered."

"Things were a bit hectic here."

Twice we had the repairman—

Lucian emerged from his silence. "Can I come up and be with you now?" he asked tremulously.

I hesitated.

So I'm thinking, how am I supposed to know from an oven?

"No, you better not."

"God, I could kill myself."

Tears started to my eyes, which annoyed me because my eyes were already swollen and tender. I concentrated on looking out the window. The sky was an Ektachrome blue. A hard wind battered the birches.

. . . in the switch, not the thermostat . . .

"Don't do that," I said finally.

"I'm going to move back in with Ivory," he blurted out.

"I should jolly well think so."

"I love you so much Melanie; try not to turn against me."

Do you get any picture at all? At the other end of the kitchen the refrigerator shuddered and started to hum.

"I guess I better go now, Lucian."

"Will you let me call you later?"

I don't know, RCA I think. You want me to look?

"Let me call you," I said.

"Ivory really loves me I think. That's why I'm going back to him."

"That's neat Lucian."

"When are you coming to New York?"

What, like snow, or like skipping?

"I really don't know."

"Melanie, I didn't mean to fuck up like this. God, I'm sorry. I thought I was just missing the wedding—"

You have rabbit ears? asked the little voice clearly, then disappeared completely.

"Forget it."

"I can't forget it. Please, Melanie."

"Can we leave it alone for now?"

"Okay. Do you have Ivory's phone number?"

"Yes."

"Will you promise to call me soon? I can—"

"Okay." I hung up.

I spent that evening under an extra glaze of pain, like a clumsy ceramic pot: a bright and suffocating glaze on thick, stupid clay. When pain threatens to overwhelm me I crawl off alone, like an animal. I curl up and hide and don't let myself think till the first shock sinks through me. By night-time, six or seven hours later, I felt well enough to remember myself again. Lucian had asked an interesting question: When was I going back to New York? For the first time in days I remembered Helicon. I wondered if Patty Bates had been trying to find me. My contract was due to expire in a week. Had I told her I wanted to record? I had, hadn't I? Sometimes my dreams are so vivid I have to remind myself later in the day that the events that occurred in them never took place in the real world. Now I felt as if these real events of my life belonged to the world of my dreams. I searched for material evidence. The songs. Rehearsals. Lucian coached me. He didn't show up . . . Yes, real. The showcase; Jules; that A and R man. Did I want to perform then? Truly? I did. I must attend to all this in that case. I must call—in the morning . . .

But I couldn't go home unless Megan was taken care of. I couldn't leave until I knew Donald was himself again. The fact of his having been cut out of Mother's will seemed to have washed right over him, though it was a cruel retaliation. I'd told him Sunday evening he and Megan were to live at Milk Lake as long as they wanted; but I didn't get the idea he was terribly interested. Late Tuesday night I forced myself to go into the sitting room to talk to him.

He was crunched up sideways on the Victorian love seat, facing the wall of windows that look out on the lake. He was so small he hardly took up half the couch. The long salmon-pink curtains, which my mother always drew (or rather, had Sharon draw) at dusk still stood open; but the night was dark and the windows only so many squares of black ranged on a wall of white. A yellow lamp hanging beside the love seat seemed to burn twice, its image suspended in the square behind Donald's head like a small ornate moon. Donald's injured hand lay limp in his lap, the burn mark no longer red and angry but an ugly pink, like the sofa and the drapes. His eyes, raw and flaky at the edges, rested on a point in the air about three feet before him. There was a kind of creeping incoherence in his features, as if they were shifting around on his face. I pulled the curtains shut.

"Donald?"

He didn't move.

"Can I talk to you?" I sat down on a wicker chair across from him, a little irritated already by his unresponsiveness.

"Donald?"

"Yes?" The green eyes rolled toward me. He smiled. "What can I do for you?"

This was more promising. "I wanted to talk to you about going home. Me going home, I mean."

"Oh no."

"Excuse me?"

"What? No, you go ahead," he said.

This was not promising. I recommenced. "It's getting to be time for me to go back to New York, but I want to make sure before I go you'll be able to take care of Megan. Okay?"

There was a long pause. "Having children in this world," Donald said deliberately, "is answering a question with a question."

"Huh?"

"God seduces us with beauty."

"What? Donald?"

"Big guy, God," he said, laughing. "Big bucks. Strings us out and thinks we can't leave, the lousy pusher. Don't you think?"

"Donald—" I'm recording word for word as nearly as I can recall it exactly what Donald said then. It didn't make sense to me but I knew it did to him. That was the only reason I didn't just leave right away.

"Why does a priest become a priest?" he asked, as if playfully.

"Why?"

"Because he's stirred by sin."

"Donald, what are you talking about?"

He laughed, reaching his left hand out for mine and at last looking into my eyes. "People are so little like one another."

I agreed.

"No, even less than you think. Take Sharon. She doesn't love me."

"Oh I'm sure—"

"No, I always knew it. She never denied it."

I said "Oh?" encouragingly because at least he was talking about something recognizable.

"I liked her for that."

"Did you?"

"Of course, we never told anyone. To err is human," he added suddenly. He looked down at his hand.

"Donald?"

Donald started to cry.

"Oh I can't face this," I said in despair. What Donald was telling me, all this confusion, was his nightmare and none of my own. I didn't want to hear his confessions. I wanted to sleep. "Let's talk tomorrow, okay?"

"Okay." He stood up. "Tomorrow and tomorrow and—um, yesterday." His tears stopped. He mumbled, laughing a little, "'There would have been a time for such a word.'"

"Do you want a Dalmane maybe? We all need some sleep." We walked toward the staircase together.

"No thank you."

"Sure?"

He answered emphatically, "Quite sure."

"Then good-night." He trailed after me up the stairs and I heard his bedroom door shut as I hit the bathroom. Megan was already sleeping.

In bed I kept thinking of Lucian. I tried using Helicon to shove him out of my head, but suddenly there he would be again . . . When I got tired of this seesaw I jumped onto another: me and my mother. When all this jollity began to pall I decided I needed a Dalmane myself (Benjy had left some for me Sunday afternoon) and went out to the bathroom to get it. A dim line of light still shone from under Donald's door. I thought maybe he couldn't sleep after all either and knocked quietly, Dalmanes in hand. There was a long ragged scraping noise, then silence. "Donald?"

No answer. What was the scraping then?

"Donald? Are you up?"

Nothing. Noiselessly I tried the doorknob. It turned, but the door didn't yield. Locked. I said, more loudly, "Donald?"

My voice sounded odd in the still house. I got a little frightened. I knocked sharply, calling his name louder. I didn't want to wake Megan, whose room was only a few feet away, but Donald's silence was ominous. "Donald?" I dropped the pills and banged on the door with the flat of my hand. "Let me in."

Then I wasted half a minute or more trying to push the door open, lock and all, with my hip and shoulder. It wasn't one of those baby locks with a hole in the knob for a hairpin; it was a real old-fashioned bolt-and-key affair. And the door was heavy, solid and high. It wouldn't yield. "Jesus Christ." First I felt a shiver of panic; then adrenalin shot through me like fire and I gave myself to the emergency. "Donald!" I pounded the door and kicked it. Megan came into the hall in her nightgown.

"Megan, is there an ax in the house, do you know?"

"Yes, by the fire extinguisher."

"Get it. Run, get it. It's important. Bring it here."

She stared at me for an instant, then turned and took off. I pounded and yelled at the door all the time she was gone. If Donald had made a sound I probably wouldn't have heard him. At last Megan came back up the stairs, dragging a huge old ax behind her like Christopher Robin dragging Pooh. Its heavy head bump-bump-bumped the wooden risers just as my mother's had done, only in the other direction. Megan dropped the ax at my bare feet. "Go down to the kitchen and call an ambulance," I said. "Go ahead." My fear was that Donald had hanged himself, and that the scraping I'd heard was his foot kicking a chair away. I didn't think I could quite bear to see that; but I knew Megan must not, so I banished her. "Don't come back," I yelled as she bolted away again. "Don't come up here till I tell you to. Sweetheart."

I hurled this last at her and turned my attention to the ax. I hadn't touched an ax since childhood. The handle of this one was smooth and dark from generations of hands. I recognized it suddenly: it was the same Iris had once used to teach me how to chop firewood. I bent over it, wrapping my hands around the haft, forcing myself to hold the extreme end, to get the full weight of the head. I'm scared of axes—and knives, and saws, anything that severs—but especially axes. What they cut and whether for good or evil is nothing to them. The old wood settled smoothly into my grip. I shouted, "Donald, I'm chopping your door down. Get back from it." I straightened and heaved the ax up over my head, standing back from the door. For a moment it hung awkwardly behind me. I glued my eyes to a spot near the knob, leaned back—the heavy ax shifted and pulled in my hands—and, clenching my teeth, swung it through a high arc smashing down into the door. It stuck there. With both hands I wiggled the cold blade out, cursing, and started again. I was hoping to make a hole near the key so I could put my hand through and turn it, but somehow the ax got the better of me. Some brutal instinct in me

201

connected with it. I wanted to chop the whole door down. I filled it with random gashes and holes. I hated it: it was all doors to me. At last, more by luck than design, the lock came away from the frame—I remember the startled look of the splintered wood exposed to light for the first time— and the shattered door swung open on its hinges. I laid down the ax. Holding my breath I stepped into the room.

On the floor, at the center of an old hooked carpet, lay Donald, curled like a worm. He had not hanged himself. He'd taken Seconals, plenty of them. The bottle and a few scattered pills littered the floor beside him. I knew where he'd gotten them without looking: Seconal was my mother's drug of choice.

SEVENTEEN

❦

No thanks to himself Donald was alive. The paramedics who brought the ambulance (not Steve and his friend; this ambulance came from the hospital) told me he certainly would have died if I hadn't interrupted him. Fortunately one of the things you learn in the music industry is when and how to induce vomiting. I shouted to Megan to bring up some warm salt water. She came, balancing two glasses and trying not to trip on her long nightgown. I poured a glass into Donald's throat. I lifted his head and chest up, jerked him around, hit his face, punched him—anything to keep him aware of sensation. Then I shoved my fingers into the back of his mouth and made him gag. Megan retreated to the wrecked doorway, still holding a glass of salt water, wide-eyed and silent.

I guess the adrenalin rush was still at work inside me, or maybe I was just angry; for whatever reason, I enjoyed pummeling Donald. "You don't get out of it this easy," I kept muttering. "You move." He wasn't even unconscious, which really bothered me. The whole time I'd been chopping the door down he'd just been lying there listening to me. He could have said something if he'd tried—moaned at least, or kicked the wastebasket again (that was the long scrape I'd heard, his foot knocking over the wastebasket) but he was busy—calling Death soft names in many a musèd rhyme, I suppose, or something similar. I couldn't make him throw up much but the paramedics got him going. Then they took him to the hospital to have his stomach pumped.

I turned my attention to Megan. She was too much the practiced stoic to scream or cry or have a fit when he'd gone, but she remained standing silently in the front hallway, arms wrapped around her thin, nightgowned chest, watching to see what I would do. It was two in the morning now. My first idea was to give her some hot milk or even a Dalmane, take her to bed with me and not let her alone till the night was far from us. Then I had a better thought. Donald's room was a shambles. "Let's clean it up before we go to sleep," I said.

She stared at me.

"Come on into the kitchen. Daddy's all right now. Let's clean up his room, okay? Come help me carry the Ajax and stuff."

I loaded her arms with basins and paper towels and cleansers; I took the broom and a dustpan, a mop, anything I could get my hands on. Armed, we marched up the stairs again. There was vomit all over the place; the room stank. I opened the windows onto the misty night. Megan hung back in the ruined doorway.

"Come on. We're going to have to look after your daddy for a while I think. We might as well get started."

I tackled the worst of the mess myself but assigned her plenty of chores and errands. My hope was that the cleaning up would prove just as lengthy and strange and exhausting as the chaotic near-death had been. I wanted, for both of us, to replace the images of destruction with simple domestic ones. In a way, I was once again making my mother fall up the stairs.

By three Donald's bedroom was as orderly as it was going to get that night. Megan and I were both yawning and it was obviously time to go to sleep, or try.

"We'll sleep together tonight," I said. "In Grandma's room."

"No thank you," said Megan.

"Oh yes, please," I insisted. "Whether you feel like it or not, because *I* need to."

She glanced at me uneasily, then looked away.

"Come into Grandma's bedroom," I went on, dragging her after me by the wrist. She stood on one foot near the door while I stripped off the last sheets my mother had slept on, with their roses embroidered along the borders and their lingering odor of rose sachet. I gave them to Megan to stuff into the washing machine while I made the bed up freshly for us. Suddenly I'd had enough of withdrawal and restraint, of sealing off feelings as if they were sacred or leprous, of private despair and the kind of delicacy that leaves people alone to go crazy or kill themselves. I told Megan to change her nightgown and I changed my pajamas. Then we got into bed. I turned the lights out.

"Can you sleep?" I didn't try to make her lie near me—the bed was large enough so she didn't have to—but I put a hand on her shoulder so she couldn't help but know I was there.

"Yes thank you," she said stiffly, into her pillow.

"Are you lying?"

"What?"

"Can you really sleep? I can't." I sat straight up against the headboard, my eyes working through the dimness to make out Megan's expression. She lay on her stomach, her face turned away from me. "Listen, Iris and I used to sleep together. I'm glad she left you to keep me company now." She said nothing. "Did you hear me?"

"Yes."

"I know you want me to leave you alone."

Nothing.

"But I'm not going to. I don't know if you'll believe this, but it's not always best to be alone. Okay? I've been alone a lot and you can take my word for it: it doesn't work very well. There are things going on around here no one can live with by themselves. Not me, not you. Do you hear me?"

She mumbled yes.

"Give it a couple of years." I lay down again. The room was absorbed in shadow in spite of the wide banks of windows. I reached my hand out again and rested it across Megan's shoulders. They trembled and she tried to pull away. I hitched myself over next to her and touched her head and her back. She held still. Even loosed from its pigtails, her hair divided itself along its accustomed part.

"Listen, Megan. What your dad did tonight had nothing to do with you, you understand? He's a little crazy right now, that's all. He's going to have to get better and then he'll come back and he'll take care of you again."

Megan's shoulders jerked under my hand: she was swallowing sobs.

"Don't try to draw any conclusions from what's happened here. It doesn't mean anything about you. It doesn't mean anything at all." I combed my fingers through the back of her hair. "Just stand around a while and keep breathing, and I'll stand around with you too, and some time will go by, and after it does we'll both start to feel differently. We really will, believe it or not." Her thin back kept jumping up and down, as she had the hiccups.

"God I feel like shit," I said. Tears spilled onto my cheeks and I automatically lifted my hands to wipe them away. For a moment Megan lay immobile, apart from me. Then she turned her head in my direction. I waved at her. We cried some more and then we fell asleep.

The next morning the hospital called and woke us. Megan went back to sleep but I got up and dressed and had some coffee. About noon, when I was really awake, I made myself call Helicon. October first was eight days away. I had to explain to Patty why I hadn't gotten back to her sooner. I was going to plead nonspecific family troubles and leave it simply at that; but something urged me to tell her the truth just to see what would happen. I did.

"How awful," she breathed, my sorority sister again. "I know exactly how you feel. A friend of mine's mother died when she was fourteen."

Well, now I knew what would happen. "Let's get to business," I said.

"If you want to. Walter and Tony and I talked . . ." She went on for quite some while. This time it was obvious she'd prepared her statement before we spoke. The gist of it was that although she agreed a good time was had by all during the new songs I played at my showcase, the response to "Real Life" had been so much stronger that they couldn't help but feel—she repeated the phrase, her voice expressing both apology and triumph—they just couldn't help but feel that mainstream commercial songwriting was what I was meant to do. So they were prepared to listen, of course, to anything I brought in; but naturally they'd be hoping for . . . you get the rest. There was some mumbling about letting me into the studio now and then to sing backup vocals (of all things) for a couple of Pelion artists—why they thought this would console me I don't know—but in essence the word was No. I told her I'd get back to her.

Around two o'clock the doorbell rang. It was Benjy, come to say he'd be gone for a few days, to Florida. He wore blue jeans and a work shirt. It was a relief to see him out of a suit.

"I'm glad you're here," I said, letting him in and leading him into the kitchen. "I need you. Can you stay with Megan a couple of hours?"

"Sure. How come? Isn't Donald here?"

I told him where Donald was and why. He listened in silence. I don't think it would ever occur to a Dennison to commit suicide. "His doctor called this morning, from Augusta General. In fact, maybe you can tell me how I get there. I have to go down and talk to Donald. Apparently they don't know exactly what to do with him now."

"That bad, huh?"

"He didn't look real good last night. I'll tell you what, you stay to dinner, okay? I'll be back by five." Benjy drew me a little map and I took off, first telling Megan he was in the house. She'd come down for breakfast but had gone back upstairs as soon as she ate. I found her curled up in a corner of her bedroom. She said she didn't need a baby sitter; but I didn't want to leave her alone so soon after all this madness. Actually, she was old enough to have come with me; but I thought I should check out what kind of shape

Donald was in first.

The SAAB needed gas and I got lost twice, in spite of Benjy's map. Altogether it took me more than an hour to get to the hospital.

I went in, my palms wet and cold from anxiety, and found my way to Donald's room. The door was half shut. I knocked softly.

"You can go ahead in," said a nurse behind me, nodding encouragingly. I went.

"Oh Donald."

I've never yet seen a person who could hold his own in a hospital. Whoever you are on the outside, in a hospital you're a patient, a thing. They had Donald wrapped in a yellow gown, in bed, as if he were physically ill. He lay scrunched up on his side under the thin blanket, clutching one corner of sheet—it had a laundry mark on it printed in gray ink—and sucking it fretfully. He sighed a lot into his hands, too. At least he was using his right hand now, if only to sigh into. He looked up when I came in, his eyes full of sadness and terror.

I reached out involuntarily and laid a hand on his bony shoulder. He didn't react. "How are you?"

He sighed. I don't know what he was on—some sedative probably. It seemed he'd been hearing voices almost since my mother's death. My mother's voice, mainly, I gathered from what the doctor told me. The sedatives stopped the hallucinations.

They'd given him a private room, small but not too grim, for a hospital. I seated myself on a chair beside him, a yellow molded-plastic chair, and talked at him for a few minutes. I told him how Megan was okay and I was okay and he would be okay soon too. He only said Mmm back to me and sighed; but the slow roll of his green eyes swept over and over me like the sea. There was a mark on one of his cheeks where I'd slapped him especially hard. After a while I couldn't watch anymore. I stood up and looked out the window: parking lot. You'd think in Maine there would be enough scenery to go around, but the truth is you can live just as ugly in Webster as you can in L.A. or Manhattan. "I better go now." I collected my purse and jacket.

"I'm sorry," he suddenly said.

"You are? Don't . . . I mean, I'm sorry too."

He said Mmm.

"It'll be okay." I left. The nurse at the station paged his doctor for me, the staff psychiatrist I guess, while I sat on a vinyl couch not looking at copies of *People*. Dr. Canfield his name was, a small man of fifty or so, with thick curly silver hair and thin gold-rimmed glasses and an air of intelligent defeat. He led me up a floor to his office and I saw as I followed him in the stairwell that one of his thin, wrinkled socks was black and one was green. We sat down in a cramped cubicle. It didn't seem to me like a good place to spend a lot of time. Dr. Canfield said he was concerned about Donald.

"If this were simply a response to the stress of the last few days" (we had talked on the phone about my mother's death), "I wouldn't be so concerned. But from what I can gather these events only triggered a collapse that's been threatening for years." His elbows on his desk, he tapped the hinges of his golden glasses with two blunt index fingers.

"Oh?"

"Did you know—this is all in confidence of course, but I think someone ought to be aware—"

"Yes?"

"It seems your brother-in-law holds himself responsible for your sister's death."

"My mother's death, you mean."

"No, no. That too; but first your sister."

"Why?" I asked blankly.

"He says they'd argued that morning—"

"The day Iris died?"

"Yes. There's no substantive reality to this, mind you, but Donald insists that the milk your sister was on her way to pick up when the car struck her—"

"Milk?"

"—was an item she'd asked him to pick up on his way home that evening. And he'd forgotten, he says, because—"

"He was angry at her," I filled in.

"Exactly. Apparently it's the argument they had, mixed up with another he had with your mother, that keeps replaying inside his head, in hallucination."

"Jesus."

"What's more, the milk was for—Megan, is that her name?—and he seems to connect her with the death too—ah, causally . . ." He looked worriedly at me. "I hope this isn't too difficult for you, Miss Armour—"

"I'm fine," I said absently.

"Because unfortunately, it seems that your mother was aware of the guilt Donald felt—"

"Oh Jesus—"

"And I believe it may have . . . influenced . . ."

"She used it against him," I supplied.

"Not exactly against him, I'm sure, or in so many words . . ." Dr. Canfield took off his glasses and laid them on the desk before him, bending over them and sort of caressing their frames. He rubbed his forehead tiredly. "In any case, your brother-in-law has been living for years with a terrible self-hatred. Now it seems he's confusing the two deaths—the two women, your sister and your mother—because according to him his impending marriage was somehow the cause of your mother's . . . ah . . ."

"It was."

"I beg your pardon?"

I explained Mother's antipathy toward Sharon, her attempt to send Donald out of the country, the revision of her will, the whole story. "Over her dead body, you might say was her feeling."

Dr. Canfield said nothing but bent over his glasses still farther, as if in their tiny metal hinges an answer might lie concealed. Then he said, "Your mother must have had some childhood."

I didn't say anything.

Dr. Canfield asked if there was money enough to put Donald in a sanitarium.

"There's money."

"Then I know a place that's absolutely reliable. It's in Massachusetts though—"

"Can't he come home?"

"I'm afraid he'll only repeat the attempt at suicide."

"Oh."

"He seems quite willing to receive treatment," he said, putting on his glasses. For some reason they made him seem more dubious instead of more authoritative.

"He does?" I thought a while. "How long—"

He shrugged. "Three months? Six months? I can't say."

I got lost again on my way home from the hospital. I was trying to think about how I felt, what I wanted to do next, and my decisions about route signs and traffic circles got all mixed up with the harder questions. After I got turned around three or four times I crumpled up Benjy's map and just kept driving east and north till I caught sight of Dennison's One-Stop. I bought some groceries there and by the time I turned into the driveway at home, I knew what I wanted to do.

The more I thought about it the surer I was. I put off saying anything until I'd called Jules, though. I found Benjy reading an old *Maine Times* in the living room; he said Megan hadn't been downstairs the whole afternoon. He kept me company while I fixed dinner. I told him how Donald was and Sharon's name came up. Benjy said she hadn't been out of their parents' house since the funeral. Evidently she was still pretty shaken.

"She's coming around, though," he said. "She's talking about moving to Boston, to be near Prescott."

"Good for her."

Benjy put his arm around me. "What are you going to do?"

"Make dessert."

Megan came down and we ate. After dinner we all went out to the lake and sat on the narrow beach for a while. The water lapped at our sneakered feet. There was something of fall in the clear air and we found ourselves huddling close to each other in spite of sweatshirts and jackets. I sat between the two of them. Megan put her hand in my right pocket. Benjy put his in my left. About nine he said good-night and ambled off into the woods toward his cabin. Megan and I went inside. When she'd gone to bed (her own bed tonight) I called Jules. I phoned from the kitchen so Megan wouldn't hear me.

I told him all about Donald. "I don't see any reason not

to trust Dr. Canfield. He seems to have a good grasp of the situation."

"What does Donald want? Does he want to be committed?"

"Not committed, it's not like that. He'd just go there and—be treated." I had a cup of hot chocolate in front of me—a taste of Megan's I'd picked up—with two marshmallows bobbing on top of it. I poked the marshmallows down with my fingers. They floated up again.

"Well, does he want to be treated, then?"

"Not exactly. He mainly just wants to kill himself."

"Oh. Then he does have to be committed."

"I suppose so."

"What about Sharon Dennison?" Jules asked, while I held my marshmallows down with a spoon. "Doesn't she want to take care of him?"

"He's way beyond that. Anyway, he won't see her. She's given up on him I guess. You can't blame her."

"So it's up to you?"

"In a way, I suppose so. I mean, you're Megan's guardian—"

"No I'm not. I just handle her money."

"Well, you could help me decide anyway. Things are pretty strange here."

"Okay. Put him in."

"Just like that?" The marshmallows jumped up, looking smaller and gooey.

"For a week. If he hates it, we'll deal with it."

"Okay."

"Who's paying for this?"

"I am."

"You're joking."

"No."

"Look, maybe I can figure out some way to cover it out of Megan's money—"

"No, that's okay. I don't need it anyhow."

"Oh yeah? How are you going to pay your rent?"

The marshmallow was making such interesting white swirls on the surface of the hot chocolate I almost hated to drink it. "Well, Jules, I have to discuss that with you too—"

"Oh boy. Oh boy."

"I'm going to let go of the apartment. I'm going to live up here."

"I knew it. I knew this was coming. For God's sake, Melanie, you can't bury yourself up at Milk Lake all winter. Why should you?"

"Megan." I fed myself a spoonful of chocolate, like soup.

"I was just going to say we should send Megan away to a boarding school. Don't you think that's the right solution? There's all that money for her, and with Donald looney-tunes—"

"Jules, listen. Thank you." I set the spoon down on the oaken table. "I know it sounds like I'm making a sacrifice, but I'm actually not. You think I'm going to go crazy up here myself, right?"

"I don't see why you shouldn't."

"Yeah. Well, maybe I will. But I'll tell you something, I think I was burying myself worse in New York."

"You were pretty hot on coming here once," he reminded me.

"Uh-huh." I took another spoonful. "I remember. Now I'm pretty hot on getting out."

Jules didn't say anything. I imagined him pressing his lips together the way he does when someone he cares for won't see reason.

"I'm sorry about the inconvenience," I said. "But I will

have a lot of work to do up here. It's not like I'll be rotting. I'm going to break with Helicon—"

"Melanie," he started warningly.

"Why not? I have an income now and a house. Fuck the rest of it. I talked to Patty Bates this morning and all they want from me is more of the same. They don't care about me and I don't care about them. I'm going to work up a repertoire here and I'm going to learn to perform for real."

"You're going to have a lousy reputation when you get back to the industry," he said. "You don't just walk away from a career, Melanie. Helicon's been good to you."

"Call me ir-re-sponsible."

He paused. "Who are you going to practice in front of, bears and deer?"

"Come on, man, there are people in Maine. Jules, I don't know. This is what I want to do. Okay? You have objections?"

He said reluctantly, "I guess not. But your lease—"

"So I'm a lease-breaker. Or a dirty subletter. Ten years from now when I move back to New York we won't mention it."

"I don't suppose you've decided exactly who is going to take care of unloading the apartment?"

"Oh, would you Jules? It'd be a big help."

"I guess you know what's best for you."

This was something new from Jules. I thanked him. "I'll be down to pack up in a week or two, but you might as well put an ad in the paper now, or call the landlord, or whatever." I was getting to the point in my hot chocolate where the powder hadn't dissolved completely. I sipped it. It was too sweet to drink.

"Melanie, what about Lucian?" Jules asked suddenly.

"He's moved out."

There was a pause on the other end of the wire. "I'm sorry," he said finally.

"I appreciate that."

He hesitated again, then went on, "I got a note from Joan Dunbar yesterday actually thanking me for sending him over. He must be some hot-shit actor."

"I wouldn't be surprised."

In the morning I called Helicon and told them I wouldn't be signing again. Patty said they'd always be happy to hear what I had for them anyway but she sounded oddly piqued, as if she were taking my decision personally. I kind of liked her for that, even though it probably could cause me trouble someday. I'm all for the personal, whatever form it takes.

EIGHTEEN

✠

I FLEW BACK to New York on the second of October. Jules
had already found someone to sublet the apartment. I was
only going to pack up those few things I'd brought from
L.A. The beds and dishes and so on were staying: I didn't
need them. The apartment had been shut up for days (not
double-locked however—my first reminder of Lucian) and
was horribly stuffy. I shoved my little valise inside the door
with my foot. On the floor underneath the letter slot was a
puddle of mail, mostly addressed to Resident but a few par-
ticularly for me. I scooped them up and deposited them on
the little brick table. I opened all the windows that weren't
painted shut and sat down by the back wall of the dining
room to look through the mail. It was remarkable to what
extent the apartment still appeared uninhabited. A dry wind
smelling faintly of autumn blew across me, ruffling the
loose staff paper on the music rack.

I opened a long brown envelope addressed in brown ink,
in small, rapidly printed capitals. It was from Martin Ivory.

Lucian feels awful about what happened between you.
He says you always told him there were no rules for

your friendship. Melanie, I love him, but I don't think he's grown up enough to understand that. He needs rules. He's still learning. I know you're probably sick of him, but would you see him again? Please do. It would teach him a lot about being a friend—more than if you turned away from him, believe me. He cares about your opinion so much.

I understand you are thinking of a performing career. I have a lot of connections in that world. If there's anything I can do for you, I'd like to. You've been so good for Lucian already.

God knows what Ivory meant by writing to me. People are so mixed up, good and evil together. Martin Ivory knew how I loved Lucian, I was sure of it—if anyone knew he did, because he loved him too. So was he pretending I only cared about him as a friend in order to spare me embarrassment? Or was it convenient for him to invent this story and leave me tied up in it? Surely he didn't seriously believe my interest in Lucian was pedagogic. Whatever his motive, his tone and assumptions effectively neutralized my role in Lucian's life. As for the help he offered me, maybe (as Lucian had said) it was simply his habit to think in terms of favors. Lucian had told me Ivory didn't want him to have an agent. Maybe he was grateful now that the matter was settled, relieved Lucian was still his after all. Maybe he genuinely wished to help me. Perhaps he hoped to control me somehow.

I squashed up the letter and sent it spinning across the floor. He was right about one thing: I was kind of sick of Lucian. I didn't blame him especially—he was what he was; we all are. After a certain point, I'd asked for everything I got from him; and what I had given, I'd given freely. As far as I was concerned, that made us even. But I didn't want to see him again.

That night I had dinner with Jules. He seemed to be getting over Mother's death reasonably well. Jules believes he was Mother's favorite and sometimes speaks of her as if his loss were greater than mine. He took me to see a play about six men trapped in a buried train. Now that he's got some money, Jules is thinking of starting a theater magazine. He'll probably do a good job, too.

When I got home I found something I'd missed at first: a note from Lucian penciled in his fat rushing script on a full sheet of staff paper. He'd hung it up inside the refrigerator, dangling down from the freezer, so that it waved out startlingly at me when I opened the door. It read,

> Dear Melanie and Lucian,
>
> Welcome back from Maine.
> I hope you had a nice time.
>
> Love,
> The Refrigerator.
>
> P.S. Please feed me.

Well. He had after all been meaning to come to Milk Lake. Did that matter? I wavered a moment, then picked up the phone while the impulse lasted. He said how happy he was to hear from me. I told him to come over.

"Are you going to hit me?" he asked with a small nervous laugh.

"Just come."

Ivory, who'd picked up the call at first, got on again and

commended me for my kindness.

"I just want to see him," I said.

"I understand. It's terrific of you. Tomorrow's his birthday you know. This is the best present he could get."

It was midnight by the time the doorbell rang. I found Lucian jumping around on the stoop, under the white lamplight, a tightly furled red rose in his hand. He held back for an instant, staring. Then he awkwardly held out the rose. "I don't want it," I said. He looked disconcerted; then he dropped it off the side of the stoop. "Come in."

He hopped in after me, glancing here and there as if danger might lurk in every corner. "I brought you your key," were his first words. From a pocket he produced my apartment key. I took it. Then he noticed the open suitcases and cardboard boxes all around us and looked at me inquiringly.

"I'm moving up to Maine."

"You are?" He danced around the living room a little.

"Take it easy. I'm not going to knife you."

"I'm not—"

"Relax."

"I was so relieved to hear from you." He stopped by the piano and stood at one end of it. I stood at the other. "Are you—how are you?"

"I'm okay. A little tired."

I watched him. He fiddled with the spiral binding of a notebook on the piano, squashing the tips of his long fingers between the coils. "I was so surprised when Ivory said it was you on the phone," he said. "He thought you'd have had enough of me."

"Yes, I know. He wrote me a letter."

"He did?" Lucian's face filled at once with anger. "What did he say?"

"Take it easy. Nothing that made any difference. He just

thought I should see you again."

"Is that why you called?" he asked, rather sullenly.

"No. I don't know why I called."

Lucian trained his eyes on the spiral notebook. "I know I let you down really badly," he said.

"Twice."

"I'll never do it again."

"You'll never get the chance."

He looked up at me. We were silent during a long moment. Finally, Lucian spoke. "Do you want me to leave?" he asked.

"No. I don't think so. No, don't. Have a seat," I offered. We sat down on the floor. I looked at him carefully. He was perfectly beautiful, there was no denying that; but for the first time I saw how deeply, how painfully self-conscious he was. I'd never taken that in before, though of course it must always have been there. He had the same maniacal self-absorption that marks most teenagers. What interested him was how attractive he might be, how effective, how powerful. I was a mirror for all that, and only incidentally a person. I remember living through that particular madness myself. Lucian just handled it gracefully, that was the only difference.

Something occurred to me. "It's your birthday, isn't it?" I asked.

"Is it midnight yet?"

"Yes."

"Then I guess so." He smiled, embarrassed.

"Happy birthday."

"Thank you."

"The big eighteen," I said, raising an eyebrow. "How are things with Ivory?"

"Oh well. You know. Up and down."

"Already?"

"That's how love is, I guess." He looked at me anxiously. "Isn't it?"

"I don't know. Maybe."

Joan Dunbar had as much as promised him a part in the Lionel Smith play, probably the part Jules had in mind. It was only a question of waiting until they officially cast it. "Congratulations. I'm pleased for you."

"That means a lot to me, Melanie. I'm going to pay you back for the videotape out of my first paycheck, too. Promise you'll come down and see me in it, will you?"

I mumbled something about trying.

"What will you do up in Maine?" he asked.

"Write music. Learn to perform."

"Oh. Thank God."

"Why thank God?"

"I was afraid you'd given up your work or something."

"No, of course not. But why would you say thank God?"

"Well it matters to me," he said, as if this were self-evident. He started unthinkingly to stretch out on the bare floor. Abruptly he stopped himself, freezing mid-move to look questioningly at me. I gazed back. Then I gestured to him to go ahead. Relieved, he smiled and lay down comfortably on his side, leaning on one elbow. "I count on you to keep working," he told me.

"Why?" I shivered. The windows were all open to the night. I wrapped my sweater more tightly around me. "What do you mean?"

His voice dropped. Almost shyly, he said, "When I'm with Ivory and—those people, I think about you and it . . . makes me be honest."

"It does?"

"Yes." His old enthusiasm slowly returned as he went on, "I've always been honest with you, completely. That's why I love to be with you. And it's . . . caring about each other's work, bringing out the best in each of us—that's what you and I do for each other. I mean, that's all we have to give. People like us . . . I mean, what else do we have to give each other?"

"Grief?"

As usual he ignored me. "It matters to me that you're watching my career. I'm watching yours. Remember, I'm the one who told you you'd do great things. I even feel like," he forced himself to go on, fighting a deep blush, "I sometimes feel I'm—like a muse for you. You know? Is that too ridiculous?"

"No," I said. "That's not too ridiculous." I leaned over and dryly pressed my lips against his cheek. "Slightly, but not too."

He smiled. His blush slowly receded. We talked a little longer and after a while I went and scared up a couple of glasses and the last of the blackberry brandy. We drank a toast and later that night I played what there was of his birthday song for him. He was so young and so earnest it made my throat ache just to look at him.

EPILOGUE

✠

MY LIFE IS DIFFERENT from other lives. Megan and I get along well together. I trust her. Benjy comes over a lot.

I don't talk about myself much anymore. I don't find it of much interest. I don't think it *is* interesting. I do go on working. My work and Megan are really the only two things that interest me.

Milk Lake is beautiful. I've never been up here through a whole winter before. When the water's frozen sometimes Megan and I go out for a walk on it, clumsy in parkas and sweaters and mufflers, waving our mittened hands. Donald's better but perhaps likes his new home a little too much. He seems awfully comfortable there. We expect him back by summer though.

I find myself still plagued by loneliness. Megan gets it too. It sweeps through us sometimes as if it would kill us; but it turns out loneliness is like hunger: it subsides after a while whether you eat or not. So you can go out hunting, I guess, and satisfy it.

Sometimes I feel I'm gathering strength, or rather that strength is gathering to me. What the purpose of this strength might be, if any, I don't know; it has its own life and direction, and whether it leads back toward the world or farther away from it into myself doesn't matter to me. It excites me to feel it growing, and I'm grateful somehow. Not to anyone in particular, or to any thing. But grateful. Just grateful.

Ellen Pall, born in New York in 1952, began writing at twelve. She attended the Sorbonne, the University of Michigan, and graduated from uc, Santa Barbara. She has performed as a singer/songwriter and as a stand-up comic while continuing to write fiction. She lives in Los Angeles and teaches writing at ucla Extension.

꽃 BACK EAST 꽃

was set by Service Typesetting, Austin, Texas, in
Electra, a Linotype face designed by W.A. Dwiggins
(1880–1956). This face cannot be classified as
either modern or old-style. It is not based on any
historical model, nor does it echo any particular
period or style. It avoids the extreme contrasts
between thick and thin elements that mark most
modern faces, and attempts to give a feeling of
fluidity, power, and speed.

*Printed and bound by The Haddon Craftsmen,
Scranton, Pennsylvania. The paper was S.D.
Warren's #66 Antique, an entirely acid-free sheet.
Designed by Dede Cummings.*